WHO AM I?

AILEEN PLUKER

Aileen Pluker was born in Victoria. A mother of four,
with a passion for European and early Australian history.
A teacher for over 30 years she took up writing in retirement.

ISBN: 978-0-6455080-7-9

CHAPTER 1

The Island

'Rain, rain, rain! Nothing but rain, for days and days and days. Why did you bring me to this god-forsaken island?'

Carter shook his head. He gave a disparaging look at the shapely blonde, curled, kitten like, on the cane sofa.

'Come on Veronica, stop being so melodramatic. It's only been one extra week.'

'Well, what I want to know is why? Why are we still here? What are we waiting for?'

'You thought it was romantic when we first arrived, the sand the sea, the solitude. A little piece of paradise, you called it.'

'Yes, well that was then. This is now. Even Paradise needs a little variety. Three weeks is a long time to wake up to the same boring lagoon, the same stretch of beach, the same face, and to be truthful, Darling, yours is becoming very boring too.'

Carter ignored the barb. He wandered over to the louvered windows and peered out at the expanse of trees, sand and sea. Maybe Veronica hadn't been such a good idea, he thought, but a man has to do something while he's waiting. Still, he hadn't expected he would have to wait so long.

He was not used to waiting. For all of his 27 years there had always been someone there to see to his needs, to anticipate his wishes.

The island holiday had been Trevor's idea. 'Get you out of

trouble's way for a week or two while I investigate the situation. Mister Curtis has suggested an ideal place; an isolated, island paradise. Owned by one of the clients. Can get it for you at special rates. Get yourself a little mate and lie in the sun and swim in the sea while I do the hard work.'

Of course he jumped at it.

Trevor had been at the terminal to see them off. 'Everything is arranged,' he assured him, 'when you get to Nassau a local airline will be standing by to fly you to the island. The local man will accompany you there and see to all your needs.

And he was.

During the short flight the young man gave them a run down on the island.

'Polly Cay is a small, privately owned island approximately ten hectares in diameter. It is not accessible for large vessels as the entrance to the lagoon is blocked by a reef and only accessible at high tide. In earlier times that made it a great hideout for pirates but now most visitors arrive by plane.'

As they flew over the small island Carter had been impressed by the resort style, luxury homestead. It was built on stilts and surrounded on the ocean side by a large veranda. He visualized how pleasant it would be, relaxing there, martini in hand, watching the sun sink slowly into the sparkling sea, before enjoying a delightful meal of sea food and tropical fruits, then perhaps a stroll along the sand before retiring with his beautiful companion.

It wasn't until the plane had landed that he had had his first doubts. They seemed to be the only ones there.

'Where's the staff?' he asked, as his guide was showing him the house, the servant's wing, the storeroom, the power plant and the caretaker's cottage.

'Staff?' his guide said vaguely, looking around as if he had just become aware that they were the only ones on the island. 'Oh, I forgot to contact the employment firm. I'll do it as soon as I get back. But it shouldn't worry you too much. There's a mountain of food. The refrigerator is full of prepared meals and there are lots of vegetables and things in tins. The lady can cook can't she?'

'No worry,' Carter prided himself with being a good cook. He had perfected three dishes, one of which always drew praise from his guests on the few occasions when he dined in, and his omelettes were legendary. 'I'm quite a cook myself.' He was more than up to producing a memorable meal or two until the staff arrived. Anyway, he thought, the caretaker must be around somewhere.

But he wasn't.

It had seemed all right at the time. He would enjoy showing off his culinary skills in this first grade kitchen. Yes, it was all right then, but he was seeing it differently now.

He frowned, then flexed his shoulders to dispel a moment's doubt. No? Trevor would never do that. Trevor would never let him down; would he?

The doubt persisted. What if? What if nobody turned up and he was marooned on a tiny island with only this whining bimbo for company, a poor substitute for a Man Friday? She couldn't even cook.

Cook! Food!

When they arrived he had been impressed by the large pantry which seemed to hold as much food as a country store. Now he wished it had been twice as large. If they were left here indefinitely they would eventually run out of supplies. Then what would they eat? There were coconuts, but you can't live on them. Anyway he hated them. They gave him indigestion. There were fruit trees, but how long could you exist on mangos and bananas?

There were fish in the lagoon. He had seen them when he was snorkelling, but he didn't know which ones were edible and he had no idea how to catch or clean them afterwards. He was very fond of fish but was used to having it served up on a plate covered in a delicious sauce. All in all, he didn't know much about living on a deserted island.

'Carter, make me a coffee, there's a pet.'

The words "do it yourself" choked in his throat. No sense turning nasty. He may yet need her for more than a romp in bed and a game of backgammon. She was the only other living person on the island and he didn't think he had the stamina to be a Trappist monk. He needed someone to talk to, even if the conversation consisted of gossip, fashion and comments about the weather.

There were birds of course: birds – they were a food source, but how did one trap them, let alone eat them? Yes, he would humour her for a while. He might need her if Trevor failed to turn up.

He heated water on the gas stove. Gas, he thought! How long would those bottles last and what would he do when they ran out? Everything depended on gas. The young man had explained it all to him the day they landed – before he flew away and left them here.

He had to stop thinking of desertion. Old Trevor would turn up. There must have been some delay. In the meantime they would just have to go a bit lighter on supplies.

While the water boiled he reached for the coffee jar. He had been horrified when he first realised that he would have to drink instant, instead of real coffee, freshly ground, that he was used to. Now these same granules were like gold. He noticed their diminishing numbers in the jar. How much longer would they last?

'We'll have to go easy on this stuff, Veronica. There's only one more jar left.'

'But I can't face gin first thing in the morning.'

'You probably won't have to, darling. There's not much more of that either.'

That caught her attention.

'But it won't be much longer, will it?' She sat up. 'Carter, what are we waiting for?'

Carter was asking himself the same question. He knew what he was actually "waiting for", a plane, a boat, anything that would get him off this blasted island. What bothered him was how he had got himself into this mess in the first place?

Veronica uncoiled herself from the sofa. She had had a thought, and it wasn't a pleasant one.

'Carter,' she began warily, 'you aren't a criminal or anything? You're not running away from the law or anything like that.'

He laughed.

'No, seriously,' she continued, 'I've just realised that I know nothing about you. Who are you?'

Who was he? A few months ago, he would have answered that question easily – Carter Langford, ordinary, run of the mill, rich and unambitious. Amiable enough but no world shaker. Now he wasn't so sure. Now he seemed to have a past, a history he didn't understand and hadn't quite come to terms with it yet.

'Who am I? Well that's not such an easy question to answer.'

'Great!' She collapsed back into her chair, not sure if she wanted to hear his answer.

Carter, instead of satisfying her curiosity, picked up his mug and walked outside, onto the veranda and leant on the railing, looking at the expanse of sea and sand. There was no wind so the rain fell like a cellophane curtain, leaving small potholes in the sand. He peered through it to the lagoon where the sparkling, tinsel drops bounced off the water.

Who are you Carter, Veronica had asked? He had been asking himself that a lot lately. When does a body know who he or she is, as opposed to that they are? Perhaps it is when they become aware of belonging to a group, to a family. "This is my father, this is my mother, these are my brothers and sisters."

But I have none of those, he told himself. Lately he had found himself, talking inside his head, telling himself about this person, Carter Langford. It was becoming a habit. Perhaps it was time for him to try explaining himself to someone else. That way, maybe, he could make sense of it himself.

'I wasn't trying to be mysterious, Veronica. It's just that I had a far from normal early life. Bring your coffee out here and I will try to explain.'

'Good, I love a mystery.' Veronica laughed as she joined him on the veranda. 'It will certainly add a little variety to the day.'

CHAPTER 2

In the Beginning – ENGLAND

'In my house there were four women. First there was Minty, a substitute mother, I suppose. At least she did all the motherly things, had most of her meals with me, took me to the park and occasionally we went shopping together. The rest of the time she spent in her office or visiting her friends. She was the one who supervised the house, made the decisions. The others deferred to her at all times.

There was Elis, about 16 when I first became aware of her. She was the maid of all works. Her duties took her from bedrooms to kitchen and all other places in between. She was always busy doing something, but always had time to stop and talk to me. She sang as she worked and taught me several funny songs, which I would sing at the top of my voice as I played in my room or in the large walled garden at the back of the house. I loved her because, unlike Minty, she never got cross if I made loud noises or left my toys lying around.

Charlie, the third member, very important to me, was the cook. In spite of her name she was not a man. Her real name was Charlotte, but she thought that name too grand for her.

'Can you imagine me goin' round bangin' pots and pans with a name like that? I can't imagine what me mum was thinkin' when she called me that.'

That was Charlie. You would have thought she came straight out of a telly. sit-com. She was a great advertisement for her own cooking, round, rosy and ample of bosom. The kitchen was her domain. She even slept on the ground floor. 'Just so I can keep an eye on things' she told me when I asked why she didn't sleep upstairs like the rest of us.

The fourth person in my house was the most mysterious of all – Amah. She was a tiny, thin, grey haired, dark skinned woman who always dressed in saris. During the English winters she just wore jumpers and thick woollen stockings under them. She didn't speak a word of English. When I was very little I just accepted her as you would a chair or table, but later, when I began to work out relationships in the household, I realised that she must have come with me from India, for I had been born there. When I was very little, before I can remember, I think I used to speak Hindi with her. Perhaps it was my first language. But as I grew, I all but forgot it. I know I was the only one who could understand her but could only manage a few basic words in reply.

Hers must have been a very lonely life. She never left the house and she had no one to talk to. I don't really know what her duties were. I only know that she always seemed to be close by, anticipating my every need. She sat quietly while I played in my playroom or in the garden. When I was to go out she was always there, standing at the front door, to hand me my cap or coat, and if I ever woke in the night she was beside my bed in an instant. She was rather like a guardian angel, always there.

My house was called Beechwood. It was not a grand estate, rather a gentleman's residence. It was a typical, brick and tile, Hampshire house. It was Victorian with eight bedrooms on the first floor, two of which were my nursery and playroom, a rather spectacular staircase and a wrought iron entrance. This was my domain, my kingdom. For I was sure I was the centre of their lives, the reason for their being. Like some little sultan I grew, surrounded by my women who, one way or another, provided for all my needs.

There was one other person, an older gentleman, who frequented our establishment once every three months. He would arrive about eleven in the morning, spend some time in the office with Minty then emerge, precisely at noon, to lunch with Minty and me. After he had wiped his moustache carefully on the Irish linen napkin, he would push back his chair, hold out his hand and say, 'Come Carter, let you and I have a little chat.'

Depending on the weather, we would go into the library or the garden and he would ask questions of me for about fifteen minutes, then stand, pat me on the head with a, 'well done, young chap', and walk to the entrance hall where Minty and Amah would be waiting, the one to offer her hand, the other to offer his hat, stick and, in cold weather, his coat.

As soon as the door closed behind him the whole house seemed to collapse with relief. I was not an overly sensitive child but even I felt the tension of the visit and the relief afterwards. I did not know why but I felt he held my whole life in his hands. For some time I thought he was God.

Mervin Curtis, for that was his name, played a very important part in my life. If Minty made the decisions in my house, Curtis made the decisions in my life. Every time there was a change he was the one who instigated it. He helped me to develop as an individual, and also helped me understand society and my place in it. Charlie saw to my physical needs, Minty, to my manners, Elis provided companionship and Amah, to an understanding of mystery and a belief that there would always be someone there to watch over my wellbeing. But none of them seemed to realise that I was a little boy, full of wonder and curiosity with a million questions in my head.

None of them said, "What would you like to know?" But Melvin Curtis did.

When I first became aware of him, probably when I first began to speak more than childish babble, he started our little chats. They consisted of questions about my welfare – did I have enough to eat, did Minty take me for walks, what would I like for my birthday; things like that.

One day, when I was five or so, he said, 'Is there any question you would like to ask me, Carter, anything you want to know?'

The question took me completely by surprise. This wasn't like, "what would you like for dinner?" This was a real question, requiring some thought. I paused so long that Mr Curtis, assuming I had none, stood up, ready to leave. I knew I had to speak quickly.

'Who are the people in the photo?'

Until I asked this, I didn't even know I was interested in the two people in the photo on the small table. But obviously they had caught my attention.

'What photo?'

'The one on the table in the hall. Come, I'll show you.' I took his hand, a thing I never did, and almost dragged him into the hall, where Minty was waiting to bid him good day and Amah was hovering in the background to ward off any evil spirits that might threaten me.

'That photo.' I pointed to a silver framed picture of a young man in military uniform and a beautiful girl in a big hat. 'Who is that a photo of, Mr Curtis?'

I heard an intake of breath from Minty and a little groan from Amah. I looked up into Mr Curtis' face. He looked a bit perplexed, his brow creased in a slight frown.

He turned to Minty. 'Hasn't he been told?'

She lowered her eyes and shook her head. Amah slunk into the gloom of the hall.

'That is your Father and Mother,' he told me. Nothing else was said. He paused a moment, as if to give me time to ask say something more, but my question had been answered. I had lost interest.

At that time I had no concept of the words Father and Mother. The word that lingered in my mind was "your". So, a few days later, as we were about to go for a walk in the park, the photo caught my eye and I asked, 'Minty, if those people are mine why don't they live in my house?'

Minty reacted strangely to, what I thought, a perfectly normal question. She cleared her throat, put an arm around my shoulder, a thing she had hardly ever done before, and gave me a kindly smile.

'Oh Carter, it's a very sad story. They were killed.'

I heard Amah, in the background, muttering strange words very quickly, as if she was reciting a spell or something.

I found their reactions quite strange. The man, my father, was a soldier, and soldiers were killed all the time. I was always killing my toy ones. I didn't give any thought to the lady, my mother. I just assumed she must have been a soldier too, even though she wasn't in uniform.

If I had asked "how" then, I would have learned a lot more about myself, but as her answer had satisfied my curiosity, I was anxious to take my walk. I had a little boat I was planning to sail on the pond. That was much more important than some dead people in a photo.

For my sixth birthday Mr Curtis gave me a large Meccano set. Minty thought I was too young for such a present, but Mr Curtis said he had been given one when he was about my age and he had spent hours playing with it. Not only would it help my motor skills but might even exercise my imagination.

He was right. As soon as I saw those green strips of cast iron, with their line of holes, the nuts and screws, the little spanner and two large sheets of paper with instructions I knew this would be my favourite of all my toys. I carried the box up to my playroom. I took out all the pieces and checked them against the list of contents. I could not read, but I knew my numbers. When I had repacked them in their correct places I looked at the instructions for constructing a square. I was clumsy at first but soon got the hang of holding two pieces together, inserting a screw in the two holes then keeping it all together with the little flat piece. Then I would tighten it with the little spanner.

Once I had mastered this skill I was away. In time I had constructed all the shapes in the instructions and worked out some of my own. Mr Curtis had been right. I was using my imagination.

The next time he came to visit I invited him up to my room to see the windmill I had made. It had a little handle and when I turned it, the sails moved around slowly.

Mr Curtis was most impressed.

'You are a clever boy, Curtis. Did Minty help you?'

'No. I just looked at the pictures and did what they said.'

'Then you didn't read the instructions?'

I wasn't quite sure what reading meant, so I shook my head.'

'Can you read?' he asked, frowning.

He saw my confused expression. 'Well, we will have to do something about that. I will speak to Minty. A boy as clever as you needs an education. I think, when you are grown, you will become an engineer.'

He and Minty must have discussed my education in her office and it was decided that I should have a tutor. Why a tutor instead of a proper school I do not know. It wasn't as if there wasn't one in the village half a mile away. I knew nothing about the concept of school but, because a tutor had been Mr Curtis' idea, a tutor was employed to take care of my education.

And that is how Miss Trott came into my life.

CHAPTER 3

Growing Up

Miss Trott, unlike the other women in my life, did not live in my house. She came each weekday, promptly at 8:40am and remained until noon. She taught me arithmetic, spelling, reading, writing, as well as a little geography and history. In my naivety I had thought Minty old, but Miss Trott was really old, fifty at least. She wore tweed skirts and rode a bicycle.

I had a natural aptitude for numbers but had quite a problem with reading at first. I would look at the pictures and 'read' wonderful stories, but Miss Trott would insist that I read the little, black squiggles under the pictures. They were boring. How could you compare, "A boy was playing with his big, red ball" with "This is Tom"? It was not until I realised that you could read the squiggles even when there were no pictures and that they told you how to do things that I began to see the sense in them. After that reading became one of my favourite pastimes.

It was through reading that I began to get a concept of Family and the part Fathers and Mothers played in it. For the first time in my life I felt deprived. I was loved and well cared for, but I missed the things fathers and mothers did with and for their children.

I had quite enjoyed the idea that I had a soldier father, even if he were dead. It was much better than having one who was a bank manager, or a shop keeper, like some of the boys in the stories did. But now I began to realise that they were expected to play a more important part in a boy's life than to just be there.

At first, I was angry. Why couldn't I have parents like all the children in the stories? I took my anger out on the others in my house, particularly poor Amah. I was disruptive and disobedient. I would sulk and refuse all their attempts to cajole me. Minty thought I might be sick and called a doctor, but he found nothing wrong with me and told her to just ignore me, it was a phase I was going through. From the way he looked at me, I think he would have liked to have prescribed a good smack.

I soon realised that my attitude was only making me more miserable so I made up a story about my parents to justify their absence. I could still see ruins from the bombings that had devastated England during the Second World War, even though it was now 1956, so I made up a wonderful story about my mother and father being brave fighters who had selflessly given their lives to save others.

The actual events varied, depending on what I was reading, but always they were the heroes. It was always my father who performed the brave deeds. My mother just went along for the ride. Now I realise that it was a father, rather than a mother figure that I was missing. I had plenty of female support but there was only one male in my life, Mr Curtis, and I only saw him once every three months.

I stayed with Miss Trott until I was nine when it became obvious that I had outgrown her font of knowledge so, after discussions, Mr Curtis arranged for me to be enrolled in a well-regarded boy's school which would prepare me for a professional education at a prestigious secondary college.

I was over the moon when Minty told me that, after the summer break, I would be going to a real school. I knew all about schools. I had read about them in the Just William books.

Minty drove me to Bartley to buy my school uniform –a blazer, white shirts, short grey pants, ties and socks with the school's stripes, pack, lace up shoes and a hat. Except for the last item I was thrilled – but a hat? All the boys in all the books I had read wore caps. What kind of a place were they sending me to, where one had to wear a grey, felt hat with a band in school colours and the school crest?

This was the first doubt I had that school might not be all racing around with your mates, playing tricks on the teacher and cricket. Still it was much too late to start making protests now. School had been Mr Curtis' idea so I would just have to go along with it. On the first day of term I rose early, a strange fluttery feeling in my stomach. I tried to eat the hearty breakfast Charlie had prepared for me, but the food seemed to form into dry, hard lumps in my mouth and refused to go down my throat.

'Never mind it's just first day nerves.' Elis consoled me, 'Charlie will make you a special lunch. You'll be starving hungry by then.'

I frowned at her. I wasn't nervous, I was sick. There was something wrong with my stomach. Perhaps I should stay home. It wouldn't be a very good thing to be sick all over everyone on my first day. But if I did go, and was sick, they might bring me home and I would never have to go again.

At the same time I was curious to see what school was really all about. All the boys in all the stories I read went to school. It was part of being a boy and I wanted to be to be a real boy more than anything. I would just have to hope that my stomach would behave itself.

At this time of my life, at nine years of age, I didn't know a single other boy. I had seen them in the village street, even had short conversations with them in the little park but I had never had anything to do with them. All my knowledge of them I had gained from books.

When Minty and I left, to drive the eight miles to my school, we were waved off by Charlie and Elis. Amah had covered her face with her sari and hurried upstairs so that she would not see me leave, as if she thought I would never return.

Minty drove through our little village, along the highway then turned onto a narrow winding road until we reached a large establishment set well back from the road. There was an iron, railing fence all around and rhododendron bushes on either side of the drive. Directly in front of the building was a neat lawn but to one side I could see a large, black, bituminized area and to the right what looked like an oval. I was relieved. Even if I did have to wear a hat this was a real school with a playground and a cricket pitch.

As we drove up to the entrance boys of all sizes were walking up the drive or standing around in little groups, talking. The sight of so many of my own kind was quite overwhelming, but it was a nice kind of overwhelm. I knew I was going to like school.

However, my first day was anything but auspicious. I was a dismal failure, ignored by pupils and teachers alike. When you have been used to being the centre of the universe this is pretty hard to take. Nobody wanted to talk to me. Nobody asked me to play. I tried valiantly for the first hour then sunk into my shell. I sat alone; trying to munch the delicious sandwiches Charlie had made for me while, all around, other boys stuffed themselves with meals prepared in the school canteen. I would have to break the news to Charlie that things had changed since she was at school.

Disaster struck in the afternoon. Though Miss Trott had tutored me well, Latin had not been one of the subjects. I was confronted with an undecipherable book. I couldn't even read the title and it was full of unpronounceable words, pages and pages of them.

I couldn't take any more. I surrendered to despair. I could feel tears stinging my eyes so I buried my head in my arms. I wanted to have a real good cry, but I still had a little pride. I could not let them see my blubbering. Real boys never did that.

I felt a tap on my arm.

'Never done Latin before?'

I shook my head, unwilling to look up and show my tear-stained face.

'Sir,' the voice said. 'Langford has never done Latin. Should I push my desk closer and help him?'

'Good thinking,' came the answer from the august person at the front.

I wiped my face as best I could and looked up to see a freckled face wearing a cheeky grin.

'Jones, Trevor Jones.' He held out his hand.

I shook it, and smiled for the first time that day. 'Langford, Carter Langford. Thank you.'

I had made my first friend.

CHAPTER 4

Lessons in Life

After that, things got better. I can truly say that the four years at St Cuthbert's were the happiest years of my life. In time I made a number of friends, but Trevor was always my best friend. We did everything together. I could talk to him about anything and he introduced me to worlds I had never known. Until then I had no idea of life outside my little domain. He knew so much about sport, not just cricket but rugby and football. The big hero was a guy called Pele. Everyone wanted to be like him and most of us were so devoted to the round ball that we would have slept with it. Rugby was the major winter sport at St Cuthbert's, football being considered a workingman's sport, but the magic of this young Argentinean had raised it to a new level. Even the sports master wanted to be like Pele.

It was Trevor who convinced me of the necessity of having a telly. Minty didn't want us to get one because she had heard it corrupted the young, so I appealed to Mr Curtis, pointing out the educational value of the wildlife and history programme shown on the B.B.C. He made inquiries among his acquaintances and came to the conclusion that it was the medium of the future so, of course, I must have one.

A small black and white set was duly installed in my playroom along with strict instructions limiting me to certain times and programs, but soon Elis and Charlie were making excuses to visit my room when certain programs were on. Eventually even Minty was converted and a top of the range Pye was installed in the sitting room. Viewing times were extended. The programs we watched and the discussions afterwards proved to be most instructive to me. I now had access to the world.

Sport was still number one, especially cricket. I saw all the greats of the day and in my dreams I was always hitting the winning run, taking the crucial wicket and best of all captaining England against Australia. 1959 had not been our finest year but the valiant effort of Freddy Trueman at Headingly was inspirational to a little ten-year-old who had only read about the great game. One day I would be a great bowler, like him or perhaps a batsman like Colin Cowdrey.

I also became addicted to news and current event programs. Minty would always let me stay up to watch them if they were not too late. I learnt that there was a whole world full of many races and colours, that the British Empire, which was still spoken of with reverence at St Cuthbert's was fast disintegrating, and countries whose names I had been taught by Miss Trott were now called something else.

There always seemed to be a war somewhere, which reinspired my fanciful stories about my father. One day I said to Trevor.

'My father was the first English soldier killed on D-day.'

'Hang on. What war are you talking about? Your father couldn't have been killed in the World War. You're not old enough.'

Great mathematician that I was, I had never done the numbers on this one,

'It must have been the other one then.' I said dismissively. Dying in Korea wasn't half as dramatic as being gunned down in a hail of bullets by the dreaded Hun. I mulled this over in my mind for a few days, especially the death of my mother. There was no way that she could have been in that war.

I remembered the fuss last time when I had asked about them but decided to confront Minty anyway.

'Minty when did my father and mother die?'

There was the same silence then the same sad smile.

'Oh Carter, they were killed in 1952. They were holidaying in America and their plane went down in a storm. They hadn't taken you because you were so young that they left you with Amah.'

She looked as if she was going to take me in her arms and console me but I wasn't sad, only disappointed. Dying in a plane crash was not nearly as romantic as dying for king and country. I couldn't weave any heroic fantasies about that. After that I dismissed them from my mind. They deserved to be forgotten. They didn't even care enough to take me on a holiday with them.

I never really thought of them after that. I sometimes felt jealous when I saw boys with their fathers but, as I had never known that pleasure, it did nor cast much of a shadow over my enjoyment of life.

Something that did darken my days for a short time was exams and reports. The whole idea of a teacher judging my work input by one simple test paper seemed unfair. In fact, that someone had the right to judge me at all rubbed against my ego. But it seemed to be all part and parcel of a boy's school life.

I also learnt, for the very first time, about cheating. It really outraged me that someone, by copying the work of others, could gain commendation. After witnessing one such incident I was all for reporting it but Trevor advised against it.

'If you do you'll be a dobber. Nobody will want to speak to you.'

It seemed that dobbing was worse than cheating. I was learning more facts of life.

I had nothing to fear from the exams and I took home a creditably report card. Of course it was shown to Mr Curtis who approved of it overall but zeroed in on my failure.

'These Latin results are very poor, Carter.'

'I don't like it. I think it's stupid.'

'Now Carter, you can't say that. Much of our language is based on it and all professional men are fluent in it.'

'But it's not fair Mr Curtis. The other fellows have been doing it for years.'

'Yes, I see. Miss Trott never taught Latin? But we can soon rectify the situation. I'll find a young chap who needs the money and he can come and tutor you during the summer break.'

That was how Peter Harrison came into my life. His time with me was short but resulted in two things. One, I became, in time, a very good Latin scholar and still love the language, even though it is going out of fashion, and two, I learnt about romance and social rules.

To me Elis, like everyone else at Beechwood, was a constant, but of course she wasn't. Like me she had been growing up. If she was a girl when I first became aware of her, she was now a woman, not particularly beautiful, but pretty enough and in the full flush of her womanhood. She would probably have been of a comparable age with Peter Harrison.

I don't know when the attraction between them began but after a couple of weeks she always seemed to be close by when he arrived for my twice weekly lessons and seemed to linger in the back garden when he was leaving.

My first indication that anything was amiss was when Charlie began making remarks that I could not understand, but they made Elis blush. Eventually Minty must have become aware that something was in the air.

'Elis, could you come into my office,' she asked as Elis came in from the garden.

I think it was the look on her face that alerted me. Elis was in trouble. She was my friend so I did not think it rude to listen in. I slipped outside and positioned myself underneath Minty's window which, fortunately, was open.

'But we're not doing nothin' wrong.' She sounded close to tears. I wracked my brains to think of something we had done to upset Minty.

'I'm sure you're not Elis but it's the propriety of the thing. Mr Harrison is studying to become a lawyer. Do you think he is suitable company for you?'

'What do you mean?' I heard Elis' sulky reply and could imagine her hanging her head and looking at the carpet. Yes, what do you mean, I protested silently? What's wrong with Mr Harrison?

'Elis,' I recognised the tone in Minty's voice. It was the one she used when I didn't seem to be getting the point. 'Mr Harrison is an educated man. He will one day be taking his place at the bar...'

'While I'm a servant, is that what you mean?' Her voice became louder.

'I do not mean this as a criticism,' came the voice of reason. 'It's just that . . .'

'It's just that you think that I'm not good enough,' Elis screamed. 'Not good enough for an educated man. Well, if I'm not good enough for him, I'm not good enough for this house,' and she stormed out, slamming the door.

I was horrified. How could Minty say such things to Elis? I wasn't going to stand for it. I would go straight in there and tell her to apologise. Then the full impact of what Elis had said hit me. She was going to leave me.

Instead of reprimanding Minty I hurried upstairs to Elis' room and opened the door without knocking, to find her, red in the face, throwing clothes into a suitcase.

'Don't leave! Please don't leave me!' I threw myself at her as if trying to physically restrain her.

'Carter, what are you doing in my room? How did you know?'

She stopped her feverish activity, plunked herself down on the bed and, putting her face in her hands let out great, heart wrenching sobs.

I sat beside her on the bed, rubbing her back and saying, *'there, there'* like the queen in the *'King's Breakfast'*.

'It's not fair,' she protested. 'We weren't doin' nothin' bad. It was just a bit of fun. I don't even like him all that much. It was only a bit of smoochin'. Fat chance I have to get a bit of that round here. And then for her to say I wasn't good enough for him.'

'I know. I know,' I soothed. 'I'll speak to her about it. I think you're good enough. When I grow up, I'll marry you. That will show her.'

'Oh Carter, you're the one.' She gave a little laugh, took my face in her hands and kissed me. Not a polite kiss that Minty gave me sometimes, but a right royal smack on the lips with lots of feeling. I had lots of feeling too, a funny, tickly feeling way down low in my stomach. It felt so good I reached up, put my arms around her neck and pulled her face down on mine, kissing her lips. She responded for a second, then gently pushed me away.

'That will be enough for now, Carter. Let's leave that till you've grown a bit.'

'But you won't leave, will you?' I pleaded.

'Well, it's all a bit of a pickle really. I don't want to leave here, heaven knows, but how can I face her after what she said, and how can I face Peter either.'

I thought the situation over for a bit then came up with a solution.

'I know. I'll go down and tell Minty she has to apologise to you and then I'll tell Mr Harrison that he needn't come any more.'

'Carter, you can't do that. He really needs the money. He's not wealthy you know. He will be one day but now he's just a student.'

'But I need you. You can't go.'

Just then there was a tap on the door and I heard Minty's voice. 'Elis, are you there? I think there has been a misunderstanding. Please open the door. I would like to speak with you.'

She was very surprised when I opened it.

'Minty, you have upset Elis, but I'm sure you two can work things out. Mr Curtis will not be happy about this,' and I went downstairs leaving the two women to patch up their differences.

I felt quite powerful at that moment. I had made it clear to both of them that I would not have any changes in my house. I went to the kitchen to request a snack from Charlie. Running a household was hard work.

I don't know quite how they solved their problem but Elis did not leave and Mr Harrison continued with my lessons only, from then on, Elis was never around when he came.

I had another lesson in prejudice next term.

'Are you a Paki?' one of the boys, Kevin Peters, asked.

I had no idea what a Paki was. For some reason our little corner of Britain had been bypassed

by the flow of colonials who had settled on her shores after the Second World War. I had seen coloured and Asian people when we went up to town, but there were none in the village or at St Cuthberts.

'I don't know. Do you think I am?'

'Well, look.' He held out his arm. 'You're much darker than I am.'

I looked at the difference between his pale, freckled arm and my toasty coloured one.

'That's because I was born in India.'

'There you are then. That's where they come from. You're a Paki.

'I suppose I am.'

But I wasn't convinced so, that night at dinner I asked, 'Minty, am I a Paki?'

She looked shocked. 'Certainly not. Who said you were?'

'One of the boys said I was.'

She picked up her napkin, wiped her mouth and drew herself up to her full sitting position. 'Then you can tell him that you are as much Anglo Saxon as he is. Your father's ancestors fought at the Battle of Hastings. Don't you ever let anyone call you a Paki again.'

Until then I had taken no offence at being called a Paki, but now I realised that there was some kind of shame about it. I had no idea why, but I was determined that nobody was ever going to call me that again.

Fortunately, the question had only been asked out of curiosity, not malice. So, I did not have to defend my Anglo-Saxon heritage with my fists, which was a good thing. I had gloried in the imaginary bloodthirsty exploits of my father but I found I had little taste for physical violence.

I was tall and well-built but saw no reason to impose my will on others, so kept well clear of the occasional punch ups that occurred at school. On the whole they were an agreeable lot and most fights ended after one or two blows were struck.

Trevor was built very differently to me. Short and skinny, he avoided conflict by deflecting it with humour. He had a quick mind and could see trouble coming and would use his wit to defuse a potential situation. I admired him for this. I found it hard to see anybody's point but my own, and would continue the argument long after I should have dropped it. I was much slower in assessing a situation and he probably got me out of quite a few potential fights. In my imagination I was the protector, but in reality he got me out of much more trouble than I did him.

So, what did I gain from my four years at St Cuthberts? I certainly got a sound education. I did very well in all subjects and excelled in sport, especially cricket, captaining the school team in my last year. I learnt that life could be very different from what I had read about in books; that I was not the centre of the universe; that it was great to win but all right to lose too; that I could follow orders even when I didn't understand the reason for them; but best of all I learnt to get on with other boys and the loyalty of good friends.

CHAPTER 5

Me Tarzan, You Jane

Cater had not meant to reveal so much of his past but he had become lost in the narrative himself. He had almost forgotten that he had an audience. He gazed, unseeingly, at the expanse of sand and sea, still reliving, in his mind, his early life.

'Darling, I was only kidding, about running from the law. Don't go all quiet on me.' Veronica ran a hand up his back and began caressing the nape of his neck, pressed herself into his buttocks, then leant in and licked his ear.

'I'm not sulking, Veronica, I'm thinking. I didn't take offence at your remark. I thought it funny. I'm about as far from being a desperado as it's possible to be, but, and I never thought I'd hear myself saying this, I don't feel very interested in sex at present. No offence intended, nothing personal.'

'None taken.' She moved away from him and leant on the railing and watched the rain. Gone was the throaty, seductive voice when she asked, 'We are all right aren't we? We will be rescued, won't we?'

'I don't know that rescued is the right word, but yes, we'll be picked up soon. Old Trevor would never let me down.'

She looked at him. 'Are you sure? How well do you know this Trevor?

'As well as anyone can know another person. We went to school together.'

'You have great faith in that guy.'

'I trust him like a brother.'

'That's no great recommendation. I have a brother and I wouldn't trust him the length of this veranda.'

Carter smiled. 'Then I'm lucky. I don't have a brother. I have Trevor. Look the rain's stopped and the tide is in. Say we cheer ourselves up with a dip in the water.'

'Anything to break the monotony.' She moved languidly towards the bedroom but returned clad in a bikini and humming a little tune.

The island was quite small, about twenty acres, the agent had said, and much of it was still covered with tropical trees and vines. The main building, was set back from the beach and had a commanding view, made for a romance movie, or perhaps a horror spectacular. There were several walking tracks, one of which led to the air strip and another to a much neglected putting green. There was a track around the island but much of it only accessible at low tide. In front of the house was a wide sandy beach, beyond which a beautiful, blue lagoon provided a place for swimming and exploring the reef. At the far end was a break where white capped waves splashed their way over the bar and swelled and dipped on their journey towards the sandy beach.

Carter walked to the little room where masks, snorkels and flippers were kept along with spear guns and fishing tackle. He hadn't made any attempt at fishing till now, but thought it might be worth learning before it became a necessity.

While Veronica swam lazily, occasionally diving to investigate something that interested her, Carter stood, in knee deep water trying to learn the rudiments of using a spear gun.

When he felt he had acquired enough skill he headed into deep water in search of prey. His attempts at spearing passing fish were a complete disaster so he decided to find a stationary one. He spotted a fish lying on the bottom. It looked enormous through his mask. Surely he could hit a target that big.

He floated motionless above it, aimed and pulled the trigger. There was a flurry of sand, the fish disappeared and the prongs of his spear were firmly imbedded in the sandy bottom. He was disappointed. He was sure he had nailed it. Still, it was his first attempt. He would do better next time.

But next time, after a similar result he surfaced to find Veronica treading water and laughing at him.

'You don't know much about spear fishing, do you?'

'No.' He was angry. He was not used to being laughed at. 'Can you do any better?'

'Give me the gun.'

She swam around for a time then dived and when she surfaced a large, spiny fish was firmly trapped in the spikes.

He was amazed, so amazed that he forgot to feel insulted. That a clinging, helpless ignoramus like Veronica could do so effortlessly something he could not, simply amazed him.

'Veronica, you're a wonder.' He swam over to her, encircled her in his arms and kissed her passionately. She wound her legs around his waist, and this time he did feel like it.

Later, lying side by side on the sand he asked, 'Where did you learn to do that? Fish, I mean?'

'From one of my gentleman friends. You're not the first one to wiz me off to an island, you know. But you are certainly the nicest.'

She reached across and took his hand and they lay, for some time, just holding hands, happy in each other's company.

For the rest of the day they forgot their worries. They read, walked and ate. Veronica proved that she could indeed cook. She made pancakes and a fruit drink.

Carter complimented her. 'You're full of surprises today.

'There's a lot more to me than you think. I don't fire all my ammunition off in the first round.'

'You think this might be a long engagement then?'

'Just wait and see. You might finish up, "Me Tarzan, you Jane" yet.'

'Better than "Me Robinson Crusoe".'

They relaxed on cane chairs, surveying the sunset.

'Carter, who owns this island?'

'I'm beginning to think that maybe I do. Though it could well be the property of the Honourable Ponsemby Neighsmith.'

'The Honourable Ponce? How do you know him? No, don't tell me. You went to school with him too.'

'Got it in one.'

At the beginning of the school year in 1962, I began the second phase of my education, as boarder at King Alfred College.

Mid-term in 1961, when Mr Curtis had paid his visit, he was accompanied by an older gentleman. Though he carried a cane I doubt he needed it. He walked with measured strides and stood ramrod straight, as rigid as a sergeant major on parade. He was silver haired, had a deep voice and wore steal rimmed spectacles behind which were the most terrifying pair of blue eyes I had ever seen. Nobody, but nobody could look into them and tell a lie.

He seemed to have put the fear of God into the household, yet he was not unfriendly to me that day. At our usual chat time, which had become longer and more conversational as Mr Curtis and I got to know each other better, our visitor was the one who asked the questions. I could see Mr Curtis watching me curiously, nodding slightly when he felt I had given satisfactory answers. It felt like an oral examination.

When the gentleman asked, 'and what are your politics?' I paused, not wanting to admit that I had none.

Mr Curtis intervened. 'I doubt, Sir James, that he has any. He's a bit young for that yet.'

'Nonsense, never too young to have an opinion. Got to know what side you're on. All that Suez business and now this trouble in South Africa, not to mention the bloody Russians.' He glared at me. 'You're not a communist, are you?'

'Oh no, Sir.' I was shocked that he would even ask.

'Still believe in the British Empire?'

'Oh yes, Sir.' I was quite emphatic about that. It might be disintegrating in the real world but at St Cuthberts we knew it would prevail.

'Good man. And what do you want to be when you grow up?'

'Mr Curtis thinks I should become an engineer.'

'But you, what do you want to do?'

'Why Sir, I want to be the Captain of the English Cricket Team.'

'Good, good.' He turned to Mr Curtis. 'Well done, Curtis. I think he's developing nicely. He might do yet.'

And then they were gone. When I asked who he was and why he had come, Minty answered, proudly, 'Lord Alyward is a friend of Mr Curtis. It was kind of him to visit you.'

She didn't give any further explanation but I knew that, in some way, he was going to be important to my future.

CHAPTER 6

King Alfred's

It was shortly after this visit that I was told that I had been enrolled at King Alfred Collage, a highly regarded boarding school. I wasn't too worried by this news. I knew about boarding schools. I had read Tom Brown's School Days. But any fears I may have had were tempered by the news that Trevor would be going there too. I had topped my class and had won a scholarship but, as I did not need it, it went to him as the next best student.

In spite of my protests Minty had driven me to the college. She promised that, in future, I would be permitted to take the train, but this first time she wanted to see for herself where I would be living.

'But you won't come in will you? You won't insist on inspecting the dorms or anything?'

'No, Carter. I doubt that I'd be allowed anyway. I'll just deliver you at the front gates and drive away.'

That's just the sort of thing any mother would do, I thought.

A new intimacy had grown between us during the holidays. It came about because I had intercepted the mail and found a letter addressed to a Mrs Garner.

'Who is Mrs Garner?'

'I am,' she said, reaching for the envelope.

'But you can't be. Everyone calls you Minty.'

'Yes, but I'm Mrs Garner also, but I hardly ever use that name.'

'But if you're a Mrs you must have a husband. Where is he?'

Minty's face went all soft and her eyes had a faraway look. 'I only had him for a little while, Carter.'

'Was he killed in the war?'

'No, but he was as good as. He was in a prison camp for over two years. He came home a shell of himself and never fully recovered.'

How does a twelve-year-old respond to news like that? I had never known the man but I felt more compassion for him and Minty than I had ever felt about the death of my own parents.'

'It's all right Carter. It's been quite a while now.'

'Were you married for a long time?'

'In years, eight, but, as a wife, only a few months. We were married in June '42; he was shot down just before Christmas. I was so happy when I learnt that he was a P.O.W. but sometimes I think it would have been better for both of us if he had been killed outright.'

'What do you mean?'

'I'm a silly woman to be talking to a young boy about all this, but Brian, my husband, was in constant pain, physically and mentally for those last few years.'

'Did he just get really sick and die?'

'No. I'm afraid, Carter, he killed himself. He just couldn't take any more, so he shot himself.'

I was really shocked. I couldn't imagine anyone actually shooting themselves, an enemy, yes, but not yourself. Part of me wanted to know all the details, part of me wanted to find words of comfort to make Minty feel better but I had no words for such an adult situation so I turned to a subject I knew, myself.'

'Is that when you came to look after me?'

'Not exactly. Brian had died two years earlier. I was lost for a

34

while then, in 1952 I saw an advertisement for a housekeeper for a small boy. I applied for and got the position and' she smiled, 'here we are.'

I wish we'd been a more affectionate household. I wanted to give her a big hug.

'I'm glad you came.'

'So am I.'

King Alfred College was by far the largest establishment in area. In fact it was probable that the town had grown up around it, for it was an old and honoured establishment. It had an imposing entrance with a coach house right out of a seventeenth century novel, several large imposing buildings and playing fields to east and west. But I was hardly aware of these.

How to describe the sight that confronted me when I passed through the arch? If St Cuthbert's had boys by the hundreds, Kings had them by the thousand. As far as the eye could see there were boys, small boys, big boys, some already men, all wearing grey trousers, blue shirts, school blazers and straw boater hats. I stood, rooted to the spot, confounded by such a magnitude of masculinity. For a minute I wished Minty was with me, I would have liked to have felt the comfort of her hand.

But this I had to do on my own.

I took a deep breath and headed in the direction that the sign GREAT HALL pointed, because the instructions had been that all new pupils were to assemble there. I kept my eye open for Trevor and spotted him just as I was about to enter the enormous room. I felt a little better to know at least one face in that sea of boys and young men.

The Great Hall had a barrel roof and high, narrow windows that cast strips of hazy light across the floor. The walls were lined with dark, wood framed, large paintings of ancient looking gentlemen. The room was at least two stories high and I had to stretch back my head to see the dark beams. There had been quite a din outside but inside there was an imposing silence. I was so glad I had one friend beside me as I entered.

A small number of students were for upper levels but the majority of us, as thirteen-year-olds, were level ones. Someone had already allocated our houses so, as we were checked off, older boys herder us into respectable groups and marched us up to our dormitories. We were given a short time to check that our belongings had arrived, shown the showers and lavatories then marched downstairs and across the quadrangle to our classrooms.

There were so many of us that we had been divided, each group having been allocated a letter. I was Level1B. I would not have been happy about this as I was sure I was an A but, fortunately, Trevor was a B too. I was to learn that the letters had been given according to our surnames and had nothing to do with our abilities but, for a time, I went in awe of the "A"s because I knew I was clever. What must they be?

If I had ever questioned the strangeness of my home situation, which I doubt I did, I was now confronted with many stranger setups than mine. There were orphans, one parent, two parent and multiple parent families. There were those with guardians and others who didn't seem to belong to anyone. By comparison my life was quite normal.

Boys are very adaptable creatures and I quickly fell into the school routine but it was some time before I felt comfortable living with so many other people. My upbringing had been more private than most, so sharing sleeping and showering facilities with others took some adjusting too. Just the smell of sweat and bad breath took me completely by surprise.

I spent the first few nights cowering under my blankets before I realised that the noises I could hear were not rats but boys snoring. I had never heard snoring before.

Some of the fellows had very poor hygiene habits. Minty had always been fastidious about cleanliness and it came as a shock to me that everybody didn't bathe every day. I found the communal showers daunting. Not only did a senior boy supervise us but lots of the chaps paraded around exposing their private parts for all to see. I was always careful to keep mine covered as much as possible but must admit to taking curious peeks at others. For a while I had a fascination with penises.

I had expected it, but I still found it daunting to have older boys in authority over me. Fagging had been officially banned years ago but it still existed. Part of the reason was that the older boys had charge of so much of our lives so it was easier to toady up to them a bit, to accede to their wishes, so long as they were not too onerous. You could appeal to a higher authority of course, but that would be dobbing, and I knew that was the worst crime a chap could commit.

Some fellows were great and hardly abused their privilege. But there were others, there always are, and in Hampshire House we had one great cross to bear -the Honourable Ponsemby Neighsmith.

'Hey! You there, new boy, take my boots and clean them.'

I had been hurrying along the corridor but turned to see four older students.

'I beg your pardon?'

'I said,' then to his companions, 'oh no, a tar brush.' He walked up close to me and spoke slowly, 'Take ... these... shoes,' he held up the boots and pointed 'and... clean... them.' He made a cleaning motion with his hands.

My mind immediately said *FLASHMAN*. I would try to act like *TOM*.

I said, I beg your pardon, because I was going to explain that I have an appointment with the house master so cannot clean your boots at this time.'

'My God! He speaks the King's or do we say Queen's English.' This to his friends, then to me, 'What's your name?'

'Langford, Carter Langford.'

'Well, Carter Langford, I'm the Honourable Ponsemby Neighsmith and don't you forget it. I feel we will be seeing quite a lot of each other,' and he left, still carrying his boots, hunting for some other junior to do his bidding.

I often wondered if, had I cleaned his boots that day, my school life would have been easier, but I doubt it. Fate had set us up to be protagonists, and who can fight against fate?'

Veronica reached across and ran her fingers along his forearm. It was a lovely, toasty brown. She knew men who spent good money in sun beds trying to get such a tan. She raised her eyes to his face, such a handsome, manly face. He could easily have been a model. His hair was raven black, a little longer than fashionable, but his eyes were a deep, piercing blue. She had never thought of him as coloured. Not that it would have made any difference to her, but now she was curious.

'Poncy always fancied himself. There were a number of boys with much more exalted titles but only he insisted on the Honourable.'

'Was he a friend of yours?'

'Hardly. He was two years senior to me. I was only a minnow. But

I would have never been part of his set. First, my skin. There were many boys much darker than me. In fact we even had Africans but somehow he got it into his head that I was a coloured. He used to refer to me as Tar Brush.'

'Anyway I didn't have a title or bags of money so I was only of interest to him as someone to torment.'

'But you must be rich.' Veronica sounded worried. 'All this, your London apartment, your lifestyle.'

'There was always money, but I had no regard for it. I just took it for granted. I was not brought up to regard wealth as any great thing.'

'Lucky you. It was drilled into me from the time I could talk. Money meant security, happiness. Without money you were dead. From the time I was small the procurement of money was my duty in life.'

'And has it made you happy?'

'I wouldn't know.' Veronica laughed. 'I haven't been able to acquire any yet.'

Carter was silent. He had plenty of money. Well, he always presumed he had. He wasn't sure whether he still did. Would he be happier without it? He had no idea and wasn't planning to try that experiment at present.

'Did you like school, Carter?'

'Loved it, even the nasty bits, like Ponce. It gave me so much. I was clever, so learning was no problem. I was good at sports, which gave me kudos and I made some great friends.'

'Including Trevor.'

'Particularly Trevor, though we grew apart during our final year and lost touch for ages.'

'Did you have a falling out?'

'No. We just went to different Universities. Life changed when I went to Uni.'

CHAPTER 7

Changes

'Life really began to change long before I went to university. Not just for me but for my household. When I came home for my first term break, a glowing Elis greeted me. She looked prettier than I had remembered her.

'Look Carter.' She waved her left hand at me. She was wearing a ring with a shiny stone on her fourth finger.

'Very nice,' I said.

'Silly, it's an engagement ring. I'm getting married in April.'

'Married! But you can't!' I felt a sudden pang of jealousy. She couldn't marry anyone. She belonged to me.

Elis must have read my thoughts. 'Cheer up Carter. You'll always be my best boy, but by the time you are old enough to marry me I will be an old lady.'

'It isn't Mr Harris, is it?' I asked doubtfully.

'Heavens no. I told you that was just a bit of fun. No, my Ray works in a garage in Hursley. He's already looking for a house so that we can move in as soon as we are married.'

She prattled on but I had stopped listening. She was going to leave Beechwood and live in Hursley. My harem was breaking up and there was nothing I could do about it. It took all of Minty's training for me to remember my manners.

'I hope you will be very happy.' I mumbled, then hurried upstairs to my room.

I had been so looking forward to telling Elis all about boarding school. Not the things that I would tell Minty, but the funny things, the scary things. I was planning to do impersonations of Poncy and some of the Masters, but I couldn't now. She was about to become a married woman and she was leaving me.

Now there would only be Trevor, who I had planned to catch up with during the break, but what would be the good of that. He already knew all that went on there.

By the end of my first year at Kings there were only three women living at Beechwood. After Elis left, Minty had tried another girl for a while but with me away there was less work so in the end she settled for a woman from the village twice a week.

With my absence Minty's life had changed too. She began doing volunteer work and joined a nearby golf club so that she often went out when I came home for breaks. At first I was hurt that she would want to spend time with others when I was home. She had plenty of time for that when I was away. I could feel my fortress slipping away and I didn't like it.

Charlie was still the same old Charlie but, Amah seemed to shrink. She looked quite frail and often had sleeps in the afternoon. I realised she was getting old.

The biggest change came in my last year at college. Minty had always come up for parent's day and sometimes to watch special sports events. Mr Curtis used to come with her and once his elderly friend Lord James Aylward came too. A couple of the Masters made a great fuss of him for he was a distinguished old scholar and a Member of the House of Lords.

In the summer of '67 we were playing Woodlands, our great rivals. I had mentioned this to Minty in a letter, hoping she would come to see me play. Imagine my surprise when she arrived with a strange man. She introduced him as a friend, Martin Stratton. I had no idea why she had brought him and was so distracted watching them that my fielding was appalling. He seemed to be far too attentive to her. Didn't he know that she was my Minty and much too old to be interested in men.

In hindsight I realise that this was churlish behaviour for a 17-year-old but, when I was little, I really believed that she was mine, and though, at 17, I knew different, I still found it hard to think anyone could take my place.

Of course we had had elementary sex lessons, starting with bees and flowers then rudimentary biology lessons but, as I was at that time little troubled by sexual urges, I gave them little attention. Some of the guys were woman crazy. All they could talk about were the girls they knew, the girls they fancied and the girls who were said to be easy.

Whether it was late development or out of respect for the women in my life, I had not indulged in such talk. Living in a male boarding school I had been confronted with homosexuality, and thought for a while that, as I was not overly interested in girls, I might be of that persuasion. This didn't please me as I realised it went against the norm, so I decided to discuss it with Trevor

'Trevor, do you like girls?'

'I suppose so. Never thought about them much, not like Millard. Having two annoying sisters rather takes the mystery out of them somehow.'

'Do you like me?'

He gave me a funny look. 'What do you mean?'

'You don't have any sexual fantasies about me?'

He backed away, trying to find the right answer without offending or encouraging me

'It's all right. I don't have any for you either.'

He was annoyed. 'Then why did you ask?'

'Well, we are best friends and if we don't feel that way about each other then I reckon we have nothing to worry about.'

'You know, Carter, you are the strangest chap I know. You always analyse everything. Why don't you ask a direct question? You'll get an answer a lot quicker.'

He was right. I have always had a problem with questions.

It must have been about the time I settled my sexuality that the breast thing began. Suddenly they were everywhere. Though we were a boys' school there were women around, Masters' wives, Matron, domestics and women in the town, and they all had breasts. My eyes would zero in on them, big ones, small ones, wobbly and tight. I was fast becoming an expert on them. Sometimes, in the night, they aroused sexual dreams but other times they grew to enormous size, smothering me, suffocating me, so that I woke, covered in sweat and gasping for breath.

The most shameful thing for me was when I noticed Minty and Charlie had them too. Charlie's weren't so bad; they were more like soft cushions, but Minty's were well shaped and pointed. She had a preference for wearing twinsets. I had urges to cup my hands around those orange shaped bulges and squeeze. I was glad Elis was no longer with us. My memory of her was that she was pleasantly endowed. I never thought of breasts when I looked at Amah. She seemed so old and wizened that she was sexless.

All this sexual tension was suddenly transformed into purest love one weekend when I met Jane.

She was the sister of one of my cricketing friends who had

invited me home for Bank Holiday. She was sixteen, about 5ft 4", brown hair and had the most incredible eyes. They seemed to change colour but were mainly greenish yellow.

It was her eyes, not her breasts that first attracted me, her eyes and her teeth. She had the widest, whitest smile I had ever seen. It lit up her whole face. I spent the whole weekend thinking up witty things to say just to see her smile.

There were not many opportunities for us to be alone, but eventually we managed to find ourselves together in a small conservatory where we held hands, squeezed waists and eventually kissed. It was the first proper kiss I had indulged in since that faraway day with Elis. It wasn't a great success, so we tried again. This time we both got it right. I felt as if I had been transported to heaven. We kissed again and again. Then my hands went from her face across her shoulders and had just about reached her breasts when we were interrupted. It was just as well that we were, for I had had my first proper erection and wasn't quite sure what I should do about it.

This was the time of the Flower People, free love and no inhibition, but ours was a simple 'boy meets girl' experience. There were no other opportunities to advance it to a further stage, but we promised to write. I penned my first love letter, overflowing with romantic phrases I had read in books, the moment I got back to college. The romance lasted, on paper, for several months, but petered out due to lack of physical contact to fan the flame. I didn't pine away or anything. I just lost interest. Our passionate epistles became more and more like diary entries. I don't remember who stopped writing first but I'm sure we were both happy to be relieved of the responsibility of replying.

For me, the world at large had become much more interesting than one teen aged girl, for this was 1967!

"Bliss was it then to be alive

But to be young was very Heaven"

Suddenly Wordsworth words made sense. It was exactly how we felt. There was a new world coming and we would be the ones to lead it.

There was so much going on in the real world it was a wonder any of us passed our finals. No matter what part of the globe you turned to there was some earth shattering happening; wars in Africa, emergencies in Hong Kong, the Six Day War in Israel and the capture and death of our hero Che Guevara; and we were stuck in an English backwater studying a language no longer used by anyone but a few academics, expected to write essays on literature written centuries ago, when world shattering books and plays were being written right here and now. We were learning about old European conflicts when the greatest examples of oppressive and colonial repression, was presented to us in newspapers and television. Daily we observed native peoples fighting to throw off their colonial masters. We were all, well mostly, on the side of the colonies and we all moved to the mantra Make Love Not War, for this was the Summer of Love. A few of the boys felt so strongly about world events that they dropped out, joined protest movements, or retired to communes, but most of us just argued late into the night and sang 'All You Need Is Love'.

There were so many songs that year, but the one that blew me away was not from the Beetles but from a funny little guy from America called Scott Mackenzie. The first time I heard "If You're Going To San Francisco" I felt as if I had ascended to another plane. I was sure there would be no reason to write another song. This said it all.

I have listened to it since and can't imagine why it affected me in this way. All I know was that for weeks I schemed of ways to get to America and join these Loving People and wear flowers in my hair. We really felt that being young at such a time was to be blessed. As soon as we leave here, we promised, we will change the world.

*   *   *

'Did you go to university Veronica?'

'Hardly! I didn't even pass my O levels. I left school as soon as I could legally do so.'

'But you're not stupid.'

'Thank you, Darling,' and she leant over and planted a tiny kiss on his nose. 'But spearing a fish does not take a great deal of intelligence. Actually, I probably wasn't as silly as I made out. I was brought up to believe a woman was appreciated not for her brains but for her beauty.'

She stood and twirled around. 'Do you think I'm beautiful Carter?'

'Beautiful enough to be a film star.'

'That's what my mother thought too. If I had had any talent, she would have groomed me for the stage but, as my only asset was my looks, she sent me to modelling school. But the aim wasn't to be a great model but to attract a wealthy bachelor or divorcee who would marry me and whisk me off to a life of luxury and take mother too.

'And I am the man?'

'Heavens no. Mother and I parted company years ago when I committed the cardinal sin. I fell in love with a poor man, a struggling singer, who as soon he became successful, ditched me for someone who could further his career.'

'You make it sound as if you have lived a long, hard life, but your still young, aren't you? How old are you Veronica, if it's not a rude question?'

'It is a rude question, Carter. A gentleman never asks a lady's age. But seeing we are marooned on this deserted shore with no immediate chance of rescue, I will tell you. I'm on the right side of thirty.'

'The same age as me, more or less.'

'But in the real world, the world I usually frequent I have been known to admit to twenty five.'

'Tell me about this real world.'

'Not yet Darling. If we are here indefinably, I might tell you my tragic story to while away the hours but for now you must take me as I am, no past, no future.'

She held out her arms in invitation.

'Sounds like a good idea.' He stood, embraced her, and led her into the bedroom.

CHAPTER 8

Becoming An Adult

Carter rolled over and looked at Veronica, sleeping peacefully beside him. She looked as innocent as a child, a few strands of her long blonde hair trailing across her face. Yet, by her own admission, hers had not been a blameless life. But who was he to moralise. She had had a hard beginning.

By contrast he had had the easiest of rides through childhood and adolescence. He had not had a mother, someone whom many experts claimed is essential for a well-adjusted life, but he had had good substitutes and plenty of love. He could honestly say that he had hardly ever missed her presence. His life had been good, so he had never felt the need for her. When he heard stories about mothers like Veronica's, he was glad that she hadn't been around.

There had been moments in his life when he had wanted to be like other boys, but they were fleeting and hardly caused a ripple in the gentle flow of his years.

Even changed living arrangements had been no great calamity. He had felt aggrieved and shown his displeasure at the time, but that was no more than the grumblings of a spoilt child.

It had been during the break between school and university that Minty informed him that she and Martin were planning to get married during the coming year.

'Which brings me to your future,' she had said in her usual businesslike way. 'When I marry, I will no longer be living here.'

This came like a thunderbolt. He had got more-or-less used to the idea of her taking another husband but not that she would leave him. How would he manage without her?

'But who will take your place?'

'Carter, you are almost an adult. You have been getting along without me quite well for some time. Most young men would jump at the chance of having their own apartment. You have already chosen to go to a London University so we thought you might like to get your own place there.'

It was true. He had chosen London to pursue his career in Engineering. He was sick of living in provincial places and London was such a swinging city at the time. But he imagined that Beechwood House would always be there when he felt like a bit of country air. He saw himself with a bevy of Dolly Birds, driving down to Beechwood where he would play the Lord of the Manor and they would drape themselves artistically around the garden, or a pool if he put one in. Of course, Minty and Charlie were part of the fantasy. You couldn't expect his swinging beauties to cook and clean!

Or else, she would be waving him off as he set out on some grand adventure to save humanity and make the world a better place for oppressed minorities. Now she wanted to change everything.

Minty saw his hesitation. 'You can keep the place on, if you want to, but you will have to look after it yourself.'

'What about Charlie and Amah?'

'Charlie has been hinting for some time that she wishes to retire. She has only stayed on for my sake. She has a widowed sister in Birmingham and wants to go and live with her. As for Amah, she is too old to take care of herself, so Martin is happy for her to live with us.'

'And where would that be?' His lip curled with contempt. Where would she and her precious Martin find a place as fine as Beechwood House?

'Martin has a delightful place in Surrey. It is quite roomy, and you will always be welcome to visit us.'

'But why can't Martin just come and live here? We've got plenty of room.'

Minty smiled. 'Oh Carter, you don't know much about women. Brian and I never had a home. We did not buy one because of the war, and afterwards houses were almost impossible to get and he was so often sick, so we just lived in rented rooms. That was why I was so happy to come here. But I have always wanted my own home. A place where I could plan things, decorate the way I wanted, do my own cooking.'

'You? Cooking?' he snorted.

'I used to be quite a good cook, considering rationing, and anyway I've been taking lessons from Charlie.'

He fired my last cannon. 'What does Mr Curtis think about all this?'

'We have discussed it and he thinks it is a good idea. He said to ask you to visit him and he will advise you about getting accommodation in London.'

So, in one foul swoop he was to lose his home and his women. He knew it was churlish and sulked for days but eventually he accepted it as a reality and went to see Mr Curtis to get advice about a place in London.

During his sulk he felt doubly deprived because he could no longer go and tell his woes to Trevor. Not only had he hardly spoken to him for months, but Trevor had found a summer job up north.

He had to admit that the reason why they had drifted apart was that he had been enjoying all the privileges of a senior boy, playing sport, nicking off to the local pub and spending hours in fellow's digs discussing the world outside our cloistered walls. It was a seminal time in England, the time of peace, free love, anti-war, do anything you want, whenever you want. We could hardly wait for the year to end.

But Trevor, boring Trevor was studying. He was just as clever and had no fear of failing, but he wanted to get top marks as he hoped to get another scholarship. He wanted to do law but knew he would have to rely on his own ability to finance his years of study. Carter thought all that a tedious bore, but then he always knew there would be money there for whatever he chose to do.

The funny thing was he had never given a thought to where it came from. He knew that Mr Curtis handled his finances, that once every three months, for as long as he could remember, Mr Curtis would come, inspect the household budget and supply money for whatever else was needed. He had agreed on an allowance when Carter first came to Kings' and they had negotiated an increase each year. Yet he had never thought to query where the money came from. He had a vague idea that his father, the man in the photo, had left it to him but I never had any idea how rich he was. To be honest, he never really thought of money at all.

He had been accepted at Queen Mary University but had no intention of living in residence. He had had enough of other people running his life. He wanted to have his own residence, where he could come and go as he pleased, but he still wanted to keep Beechwood House. He discussed all this with Mr Curtis.

'You can close it for the moment and employ someone in the village to keep an eye on it. That will free up money for you to rent an apartment.'

He was advised against buying one. That would use up far too much of his allowance and lock him in to one building when he might wish to change his living arrangements later. Mr Curtis gave him the name of a good estate agent in London, and he spent a few days looking at various places before he settled on a very trendy place in St Johns Wood. It had everything a young man could want plus a view from the terrace of the Hallowed Pitch, well, just a bit of the outfield, but one could imagine the rest.

Mr Curtis approved of the choice and arranged a three year lease.

'Now, you will be wanting staff.'

'Only a man,' Carter informed him. 'Something between Jeeves and the Admirable Crichton.'

'Such people are becoming hard to find since the war. A housekeeper and cook would be easier,' Mr Curtis advised.

'No. I have had women watching over me all my life. I only want a good manservant.'

'What about a cook? She would not necessarily be live in.'

'I will have no need. I will probably eat out often and anyway, I can cook for myself.' Until that moment he had never thought of doing such a thing, but now it seemed a challenge. If Minty could do it, so could he. He had spent more time than her in Charlie's kitchen where he was often asked to cut or stir. He was sure he could soon learn to cook too.

It was not till he had his own apartment that he realised that Beechwood had never been a home, in the sense that it was a place to which one invited one's friends. Until he was eight, people did not exist outside of his household. He knew Minty went out to visit her friends, but they were never invited to Beechwood.

Once he went to school a select group of friends were invited to his birthday party each year and he to theirs, but there was no casual socialising, He went home each evening to Minty, Charlie and Elis, played with this and watched telly. In his last year at prep school he would meet Trevor in the village on Saturdays, if the weather was fine, and go for rides.

They were living in the heart of England's history. They would ride to the nearest historic spot and re-enact the past deeds of their heroes or play poacher and gamekeeper amid the yews and oaks of the New Forest. They were like boy's adventures where they played out their fantasies, but they didn't share anything else of their private lives.

He didn't think for a minute that Minty was trying to isolate him. She just didn't know much about the ordinary habits of young boys, and he didn't know any different. At about the time when he would have become aware of the situation, he had gone to boarding school. In his final years he had been invited to other boy's places but never thought to invite them to his. Now that he had a house of his own, he was determined to redress the situation.

The proximity to Lords soon paid off. In May, England had annihilated India. By the time the Pakistani team arrived he was installed in his new residence and the news had spread among his many cricketing friends so had a full house for the first day of the first test. The 'view' of the wicket was more in the mind than real, but they could almost see the score board. To learn what was really going on they had to rely on the good old B.B.C. They cheered Barrington, celebrating every run with a toast. At the end of that first day they were more exhausted than the cricketers and far too inebriated to present themselves at any self-respecting eating establishment, so sent out for take away curries. The scene next morning would have sent Minty into orbit, bodies lying around everywhere, ashtrays overflowing, empty bottles and food containers and a smell of curry that would have made the visiting team feel quite at home.

After the earlier, easy victories over India they were sure that 369 would be more than enough for victory but, as the Pakistanis kept making runs on the third day, they were not so sure, and then England began to lose wickets. The game became serious as amateur experts began heated discussions about when to declare. England had to try and make enough runs to put defeat beyond doubt but leave enough time to dismiss Pakistan. The declaration, when it came, insured a draw, but there were some of his mates who thought England should have given the Pakistanis a sporting chance.

It had been a wonderful four days, three of the guys had lasted the whole time, though others had only stayed for a day or two. As he waved the last of them off he walked back and surveyed the wreck that had once been his happy home. His man, Peters, had done his best to keep the place reasonably presentable but had been defeated by the numbers coming and going. He could see that he was in danger of losing a good man so, tired and disappointed though he was, he gave Peters a couple of days off and booked himself into an hotel and arranged for a team of cleaners to remove the mess. It cost him his week's allowance but it was worth it.

'That week was just a sample of my new life,' he told himself. *'I was like a kid in the candy shop, or a better simile would have been that of an uncaged animal. I had had protected walls around me all my life, at home and at school. There were always rules, quite rigid rules actually, when you think that this was the 60's, though I was*

not actually aware of them. I believed that I was the master of my life. It was only when there was no one to answer to that I became aware of this. No longer was sneaking out to a pub a dangerous experience. Now I could wander into any hotel I wanted. I could stay till closing time and come home as inebriated as I liked and take all day to recover. The memory made him smile. Life had been so simple then.

There were suddenly so many choices to make. Where to go, what to wear? Apart from his objection to the grey, felt hat years ago, he had given little thought to fashion. He had been aware of changing fashions but had never had much choice of what to wear. Apart from a few casual shirts and trousers he mostly wore school uniforms. Now he was confronted with a plethora of choices. Should he go for the Mod look, dress like a Rocker or would he present to the world as a Savile Row gentleman. The one style he could never see myself adopting was the flamboyant hippy style.'

This thought amused him.

He learnt one thing about himself. He had neither the head nor the stomach for excessive drinking. He did his best to keep up with his friends, but he was a staggering mess long before they showed any effect from the alcohol they were consuming. Fortunately, they looked out for his welfare, or he might never have arrived home some nights. How he wished they could help him now.

Goodness knows where he would have finished up if it hadn't been for Peters. He had come into his bedroom with coffee one morning as Carter was sitting on the side of the bed, holding his head, after another evening with his friends. 'If I looked half as bad as I felt I should have been put down,' he thought.

'This has got to stop,' he moaned.

'I agree, Sir.'

'But what can I do? The fellows keep ringing me up or coming around. How do I tell them I've had enough without hurting their feelings? Tell me what to do Peters.'

'It is not my place to tell you what to do, Sir, but I could offer a few suggestions.'

'Please do. This life is killing me.'

'Well first there is the polite refusal. Just a pleasant, "no". Don't make up excuses, they always come back to bite you. Then there is the absent reason. Go and visit someone for a few days and I will put them off, politely, of course. Then you could always plead lack of funds. That will shake off the spongers but will encourage your real friends to help you out. That could become a slippery slope though because you will feel duty bound to reciprocate and you could be back on the same old merry-go-round.

'The best thing is to take a good look at those whose company you really like and tell them straight out that you are only going out when there is something you really want to do and you would like to enjoy it enough to be able to remember what it was next day. To the rest, try and dissuade them from joining you, politely, of course.'

'I owe that man so much,' he thought. 'If it hadn't been for him I would not have made it to Queens'.'

University! How different it had been to King's. The first few days were a wild confusion, sorting courses, finding lecture rooms and getting books. Oh, how he still gave thanks to the senior boys at Kings'. Without them he doubted he would have survived the first day of boarding school. They had made his first days there so easy. All the new chums had to do was follow orders. But at Queens, it was every man for himself. Suddenly he wished he had taken up residency. As it was he was a cork in a flowing stream. None of his friends had come to Queen Marys and he did not know a single person in the Engineering Department.

There was even a bigger problem, girls. Thankfully there were none in his courses but they were all over the campus, pretty ones, plain ones, smart ones, aggressive ones and those who seemed to see University as a parking bay until they found a suitable husband. This may have been the era of free love but some of them kept their eye on the prize.

And the clubs that one could join! Sporting, debating, singing, theatrical, not to mention bird watching and tunnelling. The main philosophy of the one he joined was serious drinking. This could have been something to do with the faculty he was in. Engineers are by nature serious people. They weren't there to sit around and look handsome. They were there to learn. Their approach to drinking seemed to be the same. The aim of a night out seemed to be to drink oneself into oblivion. This was done, not by playing silly games, but a steady drink by drink, until those around you became a blur and your body lost co-ordination. He tried to go the pace at the beginning but soon learnt his limitations so was usually the first to fall by the wayside.

Another challenge was the Morning After. These chaps, after drinking a brewery dry the night before, could front up next morning full of life, their brain cells open for business. If he managed to turn up at all he would sit, head in hands, trying to still the miners drilling through his brain, unable to make even the simplest calculations.

It was not long before one of his lecturers, a decent chap, took him aside and had a little chat. He explained that he was in serious danger of failing before he had even begun.

'You have come to the college with excellent prospects, but, unless you change your ways that is all you will ever have, "excellent prospects".'

His final thought, before he went back to sleep, was to wonder again at the many people who had blessed his way. 'Without them,' he told himself, 'I would have fallen by the wayside years ago.'

Surely, he hadn't used up his quota of good luck.

Chapter 9

The Festival

'Veronica, did you go to the Isle of White Festival?'

'Which one?'

'The first. You know, the 1968 one.'

'Are you trying to find out how old I am?'

'No. I just wondered. I was there. I was 18.'

'Well, I was a little younger, a starry-eyed girl, just turned 16. It changed my life actually.'

'How?'

'You remember I told you about my mother's great ambition for me? That's where it all went wrong. I was a wild Jefferson Aeroplane fan and tricked Mother, telling her that I was going on a photo shoot. She wasn't the slightest bit interested in the youth revolution that was going on all around her. All she read were the society pages. To her the word festival conjured up a scene of the gentry presiding over a celebration of English culture. Fortunately she had other engagements or she would have come as chaperone. As it was, a woman from the agency accompanied me but ditched me as soon as we got there. I was on my own amidst all that music, marijuana and mayhem. But instead of getting stoned I fell in love.

'Stupid me, fell in love with a scraggy, long haired, guitar player with a reasonable voice and a lot of ambition. He had convinced himself, and me too, that he was the next Jim Morrison. Instead of going home I moved in with my brooding genius to a tiny bed sit in

South Kensington and got a job in C & A's to support him while he sat around tuning his guitar or composing soulful lyrics. The only places we went to were dingy cafes where other musos hung out or to small events when he got occasional gigs

'It was very romantic at the beginning. You know, All You Need is Love, and all that. I dressed from op shops and ate the cheapest and easiest food we could afford. The room we lived in was so small there was no space for furniture apart from a bed. We had a miniscule kitchen consisting of a kettle, toaster and a gas burner concealed in a cupboard. There were three such rooms and one bathroom to each floor. In spite of the lack of space we usually managed to have one or two transient musos or their girlfriends sleeping on the floor. Fortunately, because of my age and poverty, I didn't drink, and I couldn't stand the smell of dope, so I didn't find myself on the slippery slide like some of the girls I've met, but I neglected my appearance, put on weight, and let my hair get greasy and wild.

'I fooled myself for about a year. Then I began to want something more out of life. I had enough of my mother in me not to want to spend the rest of my life as somebody's drudge. I realised that it was all take and no give with that man, but I still loved him. I was happy for him when he began to get a bit of recognition. He was taken on as a player with a group who had regular gigs, many of them out of town. But, of course, I couldn't go because I had to stay and pay the bills. Goodness knows how long it would have taken me to come to my senses, but the band started to become successful. Suddenly he had to create an image and I was not part of it. So, he just dropped me.

'There I was, fat, sloppy and alone. The one thing in my favour was that I wasn't pregnant. That was the lowest point in my short life. When I got over feeling sorry for myself I picked myself up, went on a diet, and began attending a health clinic. I was determined that nobody was going to ride roughshod over me ever again.

Carter looked at Veronica and tried to imagine her fat and sloppy. 'You exaggerate surely. No matter how hard I try I can't see you fat and sloppy. You must have starved yourself.'

'Not really. It was attitude as much as anything. I had been told from childhood that I was exceptionally beautiful. Now I looked like all the women who shared the tube with me. I was disgusted with myself, even contemplated doing away with myself once or twice. Then I came to my senses. I knew what to do. I looked on my body as a challenge. I would bring it back to what it had been. Then I would polish and refine it until I reached perfection.'

'You certainly succeeded.' Carter was full of admiration.

'You say the sweetest things.' She gave him a kiss then stood up and walking to the window, looked at the setting sun. The conversation was getting a bit too personal. 'So much for the story of my life. What's your Isle of Wight story?'

'Mine's a bit more hazy, but I think I lost my virginity there.'

'You think!?'

'Well, as I said it was all a bit hazy. I had just sworn off grog. Decided I had no head for it. Wearing my Che Guevera beret, corduroy trousers and a paisley shirt, my plan was to immerse myself in the music of the moment while spreading peace and harmony to all my fellow men. But when I got there I thought I had entered another planet. I had seen the odd Hippy and Punk Rockers in the streets of London but to be confronted with then 'on masse'. There were some genuinely scary people there. It shames me to admit this, but I was not prepared for the impact of so many of them in one field. There were people everywhere, as you will remember, and I don't think the organisers had planned for such an influx. I thought, after sharing dorms with sweaty school boys, I was a match for anything, but the smell of so many bodies, many unwashed I'm sure, pressing against me, the shoving and the pushing - and the noise. I'm sure the music was great but it did nothing for me.

The two mates I had gone with were well into it, but I couldn't seem to join in. I did not feel part of it. So, I dropped back and hung around miserably on the fringes, observing the strange behaviour and dress of my fellow Brits, and felt, for the first time, that I didn't belong. This was not my England.

And then I saw a familiar face, one that I never expected to see at a gathering like this. There, in all his splendour, dressed as if he was attending Ascot, was the Honourable Ponce.

If I had encountered him at any other time I would have gone out of my way to avoid him but for once I responded to his cheery, "Tar brush, 'pon my word" like an eager schoolboy. He was with a couple of similarly dressed chaps and though he probably was very insulting in his introductions I swallowed it all, happy to feel that I was with my own.

They were slightly inebriated but accepted my explanation for my temperance and offered me a hand rolled smoke that they assured me would cheer me up no end. Now I was not so stupid as to not know what it was, but it was the first time I had actually smoked marijuana. We sporting types had scorned it. We put our trust in good, old, English ale.'

'You changed your tastes I see,' Veronica commented.

'It was a pleasant surprise. As I puffed away one of the chaps suggested I inhale. After that the world seemed a better place. The music made sense and I wanted to tell everybody how great they were. I was one with the universe. I think I must have accepted more than one reefer for the next thing I do remember clearly was waking up in a kind of tent, under a sort of loose, unzipped sleeping bag with something hot beside me. I looked down and at first all I could see was my beret, then I noticed black hair beneath it. I threw back the cover to discover that I was completely naked and nestled into me was a completely naked young girl who looked about ten.

My mind went into overdrive, how did I get here, who was she and worst of all, was she really only a child? My sudden movement must have wakened her for she sat up, gave me a sleepy smile then, almost at the same instant, bounded out of bed and grabbed a long loose caftan.

'Shit!'

As she struggled into the garment she said, 'Rocko'll kill me.' Then she turned to me. 'Thanks. You were nice,' and raced out of the tent. The last thing I saw was my prized beret bobbing along atop an elfin face.

I collapsed back onto the sleeping bag, trying to put the pieces together. I had no recollection of having met the girl or of how we ended up together in the sleeping bag. I was haunted by the look of her childish face, but hoped that she was at least eighteen. Had we had sex? I had no idea. Had I committed carnal knowledge? I did not know. What did her remark "You were nice" mean? Did that mean that I had taken care of her or did it mean that I had performed well?

I lay back trying to come to terms with these world-shattering problems. Suddenly a skinny figure in black leathers and a large earring burst into the tent, grabbed the top of the bag, threw it back, shouting 'Where are you, you dirty, little moll, ops, sorry mate,' and stormed out again.

'I had half risen but fell back in terror. If that had been Rocko then I had had a very narrow escape. I hoped the girl would be safe from him but had no intentions of going out to rescue her. A gentleman, I might have been but, I saw no sense in putting myself in unnecessary danger.'

'And you never knew; about the other thing, I mean?'

'No. But to make sure I had a medical when I got back, just in case I had caught something, then set about rectifying the other matter soon after.'

'Well, you must have been an excellent pupil. You'll get no complaint from me. Funny about Ponce though. Do you think he set you up?'

'I've had thoughts about that myself. Then I thought I was being paranoid, now I'm not so sure.'

They were silent for a time after these disclosures, each thinking of the effect the festival had had on their lives as they sat, watching the sun sink over the horizon. But when you have witnessed this spectacular every evening for three weeks it loses some of its charm. As the last of the brilliant colours began to sink into the lagoon Carter began to feel decidedly peckish. He turned on the lights, walked to the large refrigerator, opened the door and surveyed the dwindling contents.

'What would m'lady like for dinner?'

'Have you defrosted the last of the prawns?'

'No, but that won't take long. Do you fancy something oriental?'

'Sounds perfect. And can we have rice instead of noodles?' She smiled. 'You really are amazing Carter. Where did you learn to cook?'

'Self-taught. But my *piece de resistance* is a perfectly made omelette impossible with powdered eggs. How come you haven't, learnt to cook, I mean?

'I can do enough to stay alive but it has never been expected of me to cook proper meals. The gentlemen I associate with usually rely on chefs.'

Carter began slicing and dicing. He looked at Veronica reclining on the cane sofa. She puzzled him. She could play the part when required but now she looked like any normal young woman, though much more beautiful.

'Veronica, I don't mean to be nosy, and let's face it, I am availing myself of your services too, but how did you finish up a call girl?'

'Carter, I'm a class above that. Escort, please. And you would be surprised at how often that is all the job requires. You have no idea how many men need to be seen with a beautiful woman. It is good for their image. It's a great job really. I go to all manner of exotic places and have met some of the best people in society. But as to how I got to be who I am is quite a story.'

'Then why don't you entertain me while I'm acting the chef."

Veronica walked over to the bench and leant against it as Carter continued preparing the ingredients.

'Happy to oblige. You already know all about "my fall from grace" as my mother would call it, so you might as well know the rest. With my improved body I looked for better work. Being my mother's daughter I sought the places where rich people go and finished up behind the perfume counter at Harrods. Most of my customers were women but I was particularly good at selling expensive perfumes to men, which certainly helped the bonuses.

'One day I began turning on the charm with a certain gentlemen when he said, 'I know you. You're that promising young model from Jorge's agency. What happened to you? I always thought you had a bright future.'

'Well, you know how things change.' I shrugged. 'Love

intervened.'

'And did it last?'

'Alas, no.' I have no idea why I told him all this but I was flattered that he remembered me, and anyway it had been so long since anybody was interested.

'Tell you what,' he said, 'How about you and I go for a little coffee and a talk. When do you finish?'

'Same as most shop girls, six.'

'Then I'll meet you at ten past at the front entrance.'

'And that is how my life changed. Reggie ran an escort agency. He explained that it was not like a brothel or anything. All his clients were respectable and many of them would only want my company. If there were anything else involved I could refuse and, if I agreed to more, there was to be no funny business. They would all have been well vetted before he would take them on. In fact, in social circles it was a privilege to be seen with one of Reggie's girls.

I thought about it for a while, but I had nothing to lose, and the salary I could earn made it a done deal. The training was quite rigorous, like being back at the agency. We had to be conversant enough with current events to be able to speak intelligently on any number of topics, if that was required. We could also play the sexy kitten or the vamp if that was what the customer wanted but we were not to be abused in any way and sex, when require, had to be straight.

'It was not the future my mother had planned for me, but personally I think it was better. I have met some wonderful men, many of whom I still regard as friends, have been to fabulous places and am still my own person. I could walk away from this at any time and I have built up quite a portfolio of shares, thanks to advice given to me by my clients. I have nothing to be ashamed of.'

Carter stopped his preparations to give her a chase kiss on the cheek. 'I'm certainly not complaining. I would have gone mad here on my own for so long. I thought it would only be for a few days, two weeks at most.'

'Carter, you must know how Reggie works. Are you one of his regulars?

'No, I had never heard of him. When Trevor suggested I might need a little company, I thought at first he was referring to himself. But I think you are a much better choice.'

'Trevor? How does he know about me?'

'Wouldn't have a clue. I never dreamed he would know anyone like Reggie.'

'Curiouser and curiouser, as Alice said. I think there is more to your Trevor than meets the eye.'

'I'm beginning to think that too. Actually, I'm becoming suspicious of everyone.'

'Including me?'

'I'm suspending judgement for the present. Could you pour me another drink while I slave over a sink of cold prawns.'

They laughed as Carter continued peeling.

CHAPTER 10

Life Change

When everything was ready, they sat down to honey soy prawns followed by fresh fruit and the last of the ice cream. They were so comfortable in each other's company that conversation flowed readily, ranging from music and films to what the future of space travel would be after moon landings. Veronica was sure that humans would never survive in space, but Carter wasn't so sure.

Veronica switched back to more intimate topics. 'Carter, you know everything about me, but your last confession left you watching your beret walking out of your life. Would you like to fill me in the bits between then and now?

'I was thinking about that earlier myself. After the festival I went back to Uni. a wiser and more careful man. I think that experience saved me from wasting my time like so many of my contemporaries. I didn't become a hermit or anything. I led a normal student life for nearly three years until things changed.

'Tell me more."

'It was actually harrowing at the time, but I've got over it now. I was leading the normal student life, lots of study and some play. I was going with a rather nice girl called Sophie. Don't think anything would have come of it but it felt right at the time. Then, right out of the blue my whole world fell apart.'

Veronica gave him a little hug of encouragement as he continued.

'After a night on the town Sophie and I, a little drunk if I tell the truth, raced up the stairs to my apartment. As I fumbled with my keys I heard the phone ringing inside the apartment.

'Maybe they'll give up and go away,' she giggled, putting her hand over the keys, but some instinct whispered that a midnight call could be important. I took her hand away, unlocked the door and raced to the phone but it had stopped ringing just as I was about to pick it up.

'See. I told you they'd go away.' But it began to ring again.

'Don't answer it,' she pleaded, trying to stop me from reaching for it again.

'Get away.' I pushed her quite roughly. She collapsed into one of the soft chairs and glared at me, but I ignored her.

'Hello, hello,' I shouted.

'Oh, Carter. Thank God I've got you. I've been ringing all night.'

'Minty! What's the matter?'

'It's Amah, she's dying.'

I closed my eyes, a vision of a dark skinned woman in a blue sari came into my mind and I remembered all her little kindnesses to me.

'That's so sad, Minty. I will try to get down there tomorrow.'

'No, no, Carter. She's dying. I doubt she'll last till morning. You must come now.'

'Now? Do you know what time it is? It's after midnight. I can't leave now. I have a–'

'You have to Carter. She has to see you one more time so that she can die in peace.

'That's ridiculous! I'm very fond of her, but to go racing across London in the middle of the night just to ...'

'You must come Carter. She's your grandmother.'

70

I went into shock. I could hear Minty's voice calling through the phone, 'Carter ... Carter, speak to me.'

The drama of the situation must have got through to Sophie.

'Carter, what's the matter with you? You're white as a sheet.'

She stood up and came over and touched my arm. This bought me out of my trance. I pushed her away, pulled out my wallet, shoved a fist full of notes into her hand.

'Get a taxi.' I grabbed my keys and pounded down the stairs to the garage.

Some special angel must have been watching over me that night for I broke almost every road rule in the book. How I got from London to Dorking I will never know.

I remember nothing of the trip. I was driving by instinct, my mind filled with scenes of my years with Amah. I remembered how she used to comfort me at night, how she was always there to be of service to me. Worse, I remembered the times I had been horrible to her, slapping away her hand as she tried to help me, ordering her from my bedroom, telling her a boy didn't need an old lady hanging around him all the time. She may not have understood the words but my actions would have had meaning enough. Most cruel of all was the way I had neglected her in the last few years, giving no more than a half-hearted 'Hi' to her loving gesture, folded hands and bowed head. Often, I would leave without so much as a goodbye.

If only I had known, I protested. If only someone had told me. My sorrow and remorse turned to anger. It wasn't my fault I had neglected her so. If only I'd known she was my Grandmother, my own flesh and blood. I was finding it very hard to get my head around that. She was part of me and I was part of her. I had never known that connection with another human being. And now she was dying. She might even be dead before I reached her; before I could say all the things that were in my heart.

I was so filled with outrage at being kept in the dark all these years that I almost came to grief at Minty's gate, taking the turn much too fast. I slowed a little but still had to break heavily at the door, throwing up gravel and digging grooves in the driveway. Fortunately, Minty had been watching for me and had the door open before I knocked.

'Carter, thank God you're in time.' She went to embrace me but I pushed her aside.

'Where's her room?' I demanded. I had been to Minty's house many times in the past two years yet I had never bothered to find out where Amah slept. I followed Minty to the furthest door along the passage. She opened it and stood back to let me enter.

It was a large, airy room with glass doors opening onto a little patio, but tonight the heavy drapes were drawn and only a soft down light illuminated the large bed with cream spread. Propped up on the cream pillows was a frail, brown face framed by long silver hair. The bones were so sharp it looked like a dead skull but as I entered the eyes opened and Amah let out a rasping sigh and stretched up her stick like arms. My first reaction was one of horror. I wanted to flee from this human skeleton. Then I was overwhelmed by such a rush of love it took my breath away. I strode across the room and flung myself onto my knees beside her. Her emaciated, brown hands stroked my face, her eyes had a feverish glow and her jaw muscles worked as, from somewhere in the depths of her being, she summoned up the strength to say *meree priye*.

Suddenly my mind remembered forgotten words. Words I didn't even know I knew came pouring out of my mouth, baby words, endearing words I had first heard when this woman was young and I was a little child.

She sighed and seemed to push herself up in the bed to put her arms around my neck. I slipped mine under her and stood up, bringing her close to me and holding her as she had done so often to me, many years ago. She was so light I could hardly feel her weight at all. I carried her across the room, sat in a large, cane chair, patting and rocking her gently as a mother does with a restless child.

I was vaguely aware that Minty moved forward, as if to stop me, but Martin restrained her. He gathered up a throwover that was on the end of the bed, gently covered Amah's body, then quietly guided Minty from the room.

I sat, sometimes rocking her and singing snatches of songs she must have sung to me during my first years. I sat all through the rest of the night and the beginning of the new day. Twice Minty came into the room but I sent her away with a shake of my head. I knew Amah was dead but I was not willing to relinquish her body yet. In some strange way I was trying to make up for all those years when I had never embraced her, never touched her, never acknowledged her existence.

Later in the day Martin came in, stood beside me and put his hand on my shoulder.

'Come on, old man, we have to lay your Grandmother back on her bed so that the doctor can sign the death certificate.'

It was Martin's matter of fact explanation that gave me permission to give up Amah's body. I carried her over to the bed, laid her gently on the white sheet, brushed her hair into place with my fingers and kissed her cold lips.

It was done.

I walked out of the room, out of the house and up a dirt track that led to a little copse. I sat down under an old oak tree, my back resting against its trunk and looked at the world through a haze of green. I was unaware of anything for a time, then I found myself asking that question again – 'Why had nobody told me?' but this time I imagined Amah answering – 'Because you never asked.'

It was true. I had never been in the least inquisitive about my beginnings, queried why I lived at Beechwood or anything about the people who cared for me. I had been so wrapped up in myself that there was no room for others. I could still remember how shocked I had felt that Minty could have had a life before me. The story of her lost love went right over my head. I still knew nothing about Elis and Charlie before they became part of my life.

I did a lot of soul searching, sitting there and then I must have fallen asleep, a heavy, dreamless sleep, for when I opened my eyes the sun was sinking towards the horizon.

I walked back to the house, promising that I would become a changed man, that I would take more notice of the people around me. I would listen to their stories. But first I had to start with questions of my own.

Minty was very relieved when she saw me. 'I was so worried,' she said. 'I wanted to go and look for you or call the police but Martin said I had to give you time, a little space. He knew you would come back when you were ready.

What a wise man you have married, I thought. Of course she wanted to feed me but first I needed a wash and a change of clothing. It was not till the meal was finished and we were sitting in easy chairs, nursing after dinner drinks that I asked, 'Minty, would you tell me what you know about my beginnings?'

'Of course I will. I don't know everything. You will have to ask Mr Curtis. He knows a lot more than I do. I will tell you what I can.

'I answered an advertisement for a housekeeper and was told that the parents of a small child had been killed in a plane crash. The boy was living with his Grandmother in India but he was to be brought home to grow up in England as an Englishman. I was told nothing about his English family, but I realised they must have been wealthy for our wages were generous and there was always enough money to run the house. All problems were referred to Mr Curtis. I did ask a few questions at the beginning but I got the impression that I would only be told what I needed to know to run the establishment. Over the years I lost interest. Carter, I'm sorry. I always thought you knew about Amah. Did you never wonder why she was there?'

'I thought she was a servant who had brought me to England then stayed there to look after me. To tell the truth Minty, I didn't think about her at all. I just accepted her the same way as I accepted all of you.'

'It's not your fault. It was the way we brought you up. I realise now that you had a very isolated childhood. I suppose I am to blame but I assure you it was out of ignorance. For several years my time had been taken up with my husband, Brian. I never knew from one day to the next who he would be. Sometimes he was the same loving person I had married. Then he would become morose, withdrawn. At other times he would be like a little, dependent child, relying on me for everything. To keep myself sane I stifled all emotion including any maternal ones. When I took the job, that was how I saw it, a job, and you were just one part of it. I didn't have to mother you. Amah was there for that. I didn't have to feed you. That was Charlie's job and there was Elis to entertain you. By the time I trusted life enough to love you, a pattern had been set. Goodness knows how you would have turned out if it hadn't been for school.'

Carter nodded. 'I don't hold it against you for a minute. I have always thought I had a wonderful childhood. I saw myself as running everything. It wasn't until I went to Kings that I realised I wasn't the centre of the universe. But now I need to know more about myself. Minty, I realise now that I am part Indian but, do you remember telling me that my family went back to the Battle of Hastings?'

'Oh, I remember. I was angry with that boy for calling you a Paki. It was a very derogatory term then. I'm afraid I exaggerated a little but I do know that your family must have been here for a long time.'

'I suppose that's so. I shouldn't have much trouble finding them but I'm much more interested in Amah, who was she? Where did she come from? And what about my mother?'

'I can't help you there, Carter,' Minty said, 'You will have to speak to Mr Curtis about that.'

I stayed the night with Minty and Martin but slept little. I had so many things on my mind, the most immediate of which was to do, in death, what I had neglected during Amah's life. I would take control of the funeral arrangements. I rose as soon as I heard movement in the house and went into the kitchen where Minty was brewing coffee.

'Good morning, Carter. Did you sleep well?'

'Not well, I'm afraid. Too much on my mind. Minty, do you know anything about Hindu funerals?

'Nothing. But why do you ask?'

'I want to make all the arrangements for Amah's funeral.'

'What makes you think she was a Hindu?'

'Well, she's Indian, and she always had that little statue on the little table in her room where she burnt incense, and she had flowers. She couldn't be Muslim. They don't do that.

'Carter, how often did you go into Amah's room? That is not a statue of a Hindu god. That's the Virgin Mary. Amah was a Catholic.'

'A Catholic? But she never went to church.'

'She never went anywhere, if you remember. I never enquired whether she wanted to go. I could hardly converse with her. Most of our communication was done in signs. I'm afraid, Carter, you were not the only one who neglected her. I took her for granted too. I know nothing about Catholicism, but I do know that that is a statue of the Virgin.'

I had a sudden thought. 'Do you think I might be Catholic too?'

'I never gave it a thought, but I'm sure Mr Curtis would have informed me if it had been important. Whatever you were at birth, you have been brought up as an Anglican, though, I'm afraid, not a very committed one. I'm must admit that religion has been more of a habit than a belief for me. It was what one does.'

'I always thought it made me very British. But if Amah was Catholic it complicates things. I had thought that we could have had some sort of Hindu ceremony and then I could take her ashes back to India.'

'I think you could still do that. There is a Catholic church not far from here. Why don't you go and have a talk to the priest?'

The parish priest at St Brigit's was an old Irish man. He was most impressed to hear about Amah's devotion to the Virgin, mourned the fact that he had not known of her so that he could have visited.

'Poor lady, dying without the comfort of the eucharist. If only I had known of her existence. Still she had the consolation of the Virgin all these years. Of course I will bless her body and we can arrange for a little Mass to be said. Seeing you wish to take her remains back to her homeland, I don't see any problem with cremation.'

Father Keenan was as good as his word and two days later Amah was farewelled from this world with a simple, but dignified service at St Brigit's. There were only a dozen mourners, among them a very frail, old Charley and a buxom Elis, her husband Ray, and a lively little girl as pretty as her mother had been.

I felt ashamed that I had been so tied up with my own affairs that I had never bothered to make contact with these two women who had been such a big part of my life. I promised to renew contact as soon as I returned from India.

Another mourner was Mr Curtis. After the service I arranged a meeting where I could satisfy my curiosity about my beginnings.

I no longer wanted to be the selfish, self-satisfied person I had become. I needed to know who I really was before I could begin to reform. How was it that I had grown up in the heart of England, believing I was English through and through, yet I had an Indian grandmother?

I had decided I would not return to university. Instead, I would forsake the country which had rejected my Grandmother and instead devote my future to bettering the lives of the people of her land. I did not feel Indian yet, but when I arrived there I knew I would embrace this country whose history was old when England was just a series of small kingdoms fighting amongst themselves for supremacy.

CHAPTER 11

Letter from a Father

Three days after the funeral I kept my appointment with Mr Curtis. He offered his condolences and asked what I was planning to do with Amah's ashes.

'There are a number of plans I wish you to make for me Sir, but first, I must learn more about my background. Until Amah's death I didn't even know that she was my Grandmother. I know nothing about my Mother and Father apart from that photo in the hall and I've only just learnt that I am part Indian. Minty has told me what she knows, which was not a great deal. Please Mr Curtis, what can you tell me about my family?'

He gave me one of his rare smiles and I noticed, for the first time, that he was growing old. I felt an unexpected sadness. He was the nearest thing I had to a Grandfather. Was I going to lose him too?

'I'm sorry Carter. Nobody deliberately kept your origin from you. It was always planned to enlighten you when you reached your majority. First, I would like you to read this letter. Then you can ask me anything that you want to know and I will help you as much as I can.'

He opened a folder that was on his deck and took out a couple of folded sheets of paper, which proved to be a handwritten letter. When I opened it and read the greeting, I was overcome with grief and astonishment. It took me some time to compose myself so that I could continue reading, but it filled in all the gaps.

My Dear Son,

As I sit here, at 3a.m. watching you sleeping peacefully in your bassinette I wonder what your future will be. I hope I will be there to share it with you but, I'm afraid, your Old Man is not a prime candidate for old age. Still, one never knows. We are leaving with the hope that a cure can be found in new surgery which is being pioneered in America. Modern medicine is advancing so fast that we may all be able to live forever.

But, on the chance that I am not around to share this with you, I'm writing a few lines about your beginnings, in case you may be interested. Every family has a few strange stories and yours is no exception. I am not speaking about the dim, distant past but happenings in this century.

The story begins in 1920, when, in spite of the first world-war, England was still a mighty empire and India was ruled by the British Raj.

Two young men, both from good British stock, whose families had given their lives to upholding the Empire in various places in the world for several generations, came to India to protect it, to continue the work of civilizing it and to have the adventure of their lives. They were the best of friends, had been born in India themselves but spent all of their formative years in England. They were steeped in the glories of the past, particularly the victories and disasters of conquering and holding territory. They were weaned on stories of the Indian Mutiny and the Khyber Pass; but all that was behind them, or so they thought. Britain had defeated the Hun. They would have no trouble from a few black fanatics. They were looking forward to polo matches, tiffin in the mess and marrying fragile English beauties who came out to India looking for suitable husbands. One of these gentlemen was your grandfather, Roger Travis.

He married Jean, the sister of his best friend. I do not know how happy this match was but I do know that the life of the memsahib suited Jean and she soon became the centre of the 'smart set'. It probably would have been a successful marriage had not history intervened.

There was unrest in India at the time. Ghandi, back from South Africa, started the Indian National Congress with the aim of an Independent India. As well there was constant rioting between Muslims and Hindus. It was during one of these religious riots, in 1931, that Roger and a troop of Sepoys were sent to rescue a small community of Indian Christians who were caught in the middle.

Among those rescued was a beautiful young woman whose father, a teacher, had been severely injured. Roger demanded that he be treated in a European hospital and took a personal interest in his recovery. Perhaps his interest in the father had a lot to do with the daughter and in time this interest turned to love. In those days interracial marriage was unacceptable and anyway he was a married man.

It was against her tradition too but the young girl returned his affection.

His wife, Jean, unable to bear the scandal of her husband's infidelity with a coloured, sued for divorce and sailed back to England.

Roger was ostracised by the British community, particularly his friend, whose sister he had made a figure of gossip and shame. The girl, whose name was Uma, was disowned by her family because, as a Catholic, she could not marry a divorced man. Roger resigned his commission and began working in a trading firm.

In time a daughter, Zidi was born. Their life might have continued in this way but, in 1939, war broke out in Europe. Roger re-enlisted.

So many men were needed to fight the war in Europe, that a trained officer was a great asset to the army in India. The war did not remain in Europe and Roger Travis and many of his men died in the jungles of Malaya.

Now I come to my part in this story.

Roger's English wife was my Aunt Jean and her brother James, my father. I learnt, quite by accident that something had happened to her, while she was in India, but the family never spoke of it. I had found a wedding photo one day in an album. It showed the bride, Jean, my mother as bridesmaid, my father as best man and another, handsome, young man dressed in Military Dress Uniform.

My mother grudgingly told me his name was Roger then shut the album and put it on a high shelf. When I found it again the photo had been taken out. From that day on my ears were open to any little bits of gossip about India. In time I learnt that Aunt Jean's husband was Roger Travis, that he had once been my father's best friend and that they had served together in India before the war.

I was lucky to be still in training when the war ended but was sent out to India in 1946, where things were in turmoil. The Muslims and Hindus were still at each other's throats but were united in their desire for independence from Britain, so we were sent out to provide a degree of peace while negotiating a withdrawal.

My father was furious with the whole situation. Members of his family had served in India for three generations. He had become ill over there and was retired on a half pension in thirty-seven, so had missed most of the turmoil of the late thirties. To him India was still 'The Jewel in the Crown.' He still basked in the glow his glory days in India so felt personally betrayed.

"After all we've done for them," he would rant. "After all the lives sacrificed. If we hadn't held the line the Japs would have overrun the

whole country. But is there any gratitude? No! Now all they can say is "Britain Out". Well, we'll get the last laugh. Let's see how they get on without us. I never really liked them. All smiles and "Yes Sahib" to your face, but you could never turn your back on them."

It was easy to guess that he no longer held any love for the country where he had spent so many years.

For myself, I was excited to go. Apart from seeing all those exotic places where I had been born, I was also determined to get to the bottom of the family secret and solve the mystery of Aunt Jean's husband. I had done my research and knew that he had left the army and worked in Bombay and enlisted from there. After that the trail had gone cold.

I was in luck when I met an old soldier who had served under my father. He told me the whole sorry saga. It helped me realise why my father was so angry. After all Aunt Jean was his only sister and she had never married again.

'You must remember.' Kishan explained to me, 'your father was a product of his times. The English, especially the officers saw themselves as superior beings. I think they regarded us as they regarded their dogs. They cared for us but in return they expected utter loyalty. That was why it was a disgrace that Sahib Travis took up with an Indian girl. I'm not saying that there were not a many of them having sex with Indian women of a certain type. But Sahib Travers wanted to set up house with her, to marry her. Still, it was not right, what the army did to her and the child. He went back to fight their fight, but they would not give his wife a pension.'

'Hang on a minute. Did you say, a child?'

'Yes, a beautiful daughter, Zedi. She was nine when her father died and Uma has had to bring her up as best she could. No help from the military and no help from her family either. She was *disowned for living with a divorced man. Still, she has worked herself to the bone to bring her daughter up as a proper English lady. Some of Sahib Travis' comrades help when they can and the good sisters have given her a free education even though, in their eyes, she is a bastard.'*

I was bursting with excitement. 'Could you tell me their address?'

'Why would you want to meet her? Your family hates her.'

'But I don't. Anyway, the child is a kind of relation through marriage. I would like to help, if I can. Maybe there is money in England that belongs to her.'

'That could be so, but Uma is a proud woman. I would have to ask her permission first.'

A few days later Kishan came to me and said he would take me to Uma. 'You must not be repelled by the way she is living. It is the British army who is responsible.'

I had been in India long enough to know how the poor lived, but I was still shocked. Their living quarters consisted of a covered space between two buildings. Some bedding rolled up in a corner, a very small table, a box with two shelves and an iron brassier was the only furniture. Uma, the beauty who had stolen the heart of a British officer, was now a shrivelled up old lady even though she could have only been in her thirties. In the midst of all this stood a young girl in immaculate school uniform. She looked so incongruous amid all this squalor that I failed, at first, to notice how beautiful she was.

She stepped forward and held out her hand, in the European fashion. 'Welcome to our home. I am Zedi, and this is my mother Uma. She does not speak English so I will act as interpreter.'

Poor she may have been, but this girl had plenty of spirit. I think I fell in love with her at that moment but it was some time before I recognised the emotion as other than a desire to protect her. I explained my relationship to them and asked questions about Travis and his fate.

Things were pretty tense for a while but when they realised that my only wish was to be of assistance to them, they welcomed me properly. Soon I became a constant visitor.

That first night I wrote a letter to my father, telling him of their plight and asking for any help he could give.

His answer came as fast as airmail could deliver it. It is a wonder the paper didn't burn on the way. I was to have nothing more to do with those people. I was not to visit them, speak to them and I must never, never ever think of becoming involved in their lives. Let the New India provide for them.

I probably would have helped them anyway but my father's letter made me determined to get them out of their present state and give them the life they deserved. I made myself very unpopular in India and at home with my petitions, but they had no success. I allocated most of my pay towards their upkeep and, when it came time to come home I, like Travis, resigned from the army to take my chances in the new society.

By this time I knew I was in love with your mother and we were married in 1949. I had had no communication with my father for some time but when I wrote, informing of my intention to marry, I received an official document informing me that I had been disinherited, cut off from the family tree and in future I was to be known by my mother's maiden name.

This was a terrible thing for a father to do but, my darling son, it has never cast a shadow over my life. I know that to have your mother and you to love me, I am a wealthy man. I have my own resources and I will see that you will always be provided for financially. No matter what the outcome of this new treatment, *know that you will always have my love. Sleep well, my darling boy.*

This letter left me numb. Curtis gave me time to absorb it, then said apologetically, 'I'm sorry you had to learn of your past at such a sad time but, as a lawyer I am bound to follow the wishes of my client.'

'Your client? You're not going to tell me that my father is still alive?'

'No, Carter. The facts of your parent's death are true. My client is your grandfather.'

'The man that abandoned my father! Well, you can tell him I don't want anything to do with him either. If he has been providing my income, then I don't need it. I can make my own way. Thank you.'

'No, Carter, your income comes from your father's estate. It was left to him by his mother.'

'Is she alive?'

'No. She died not long after you were born.'

'So, I am an orphan twice over. Both my grandmothers are also dead, as well as my parents. The only one left is a man I despise.' I was so angry it overcame my grief. 'And who is this monster who would disown his son?'

'I am not at liberty to say.'

'Just as well. If I knew where he lived, I would probably go there and kill him. This has made up my mind. I am going to leave England. Since I have been disowned here, I will go to India and become an Indian. I will never set foot on this soil again.'

'I understand how you feel, boy, you are still in shock. But don't burn all your bridges just yet. There are still people here who care for you. Minty for one.'

'She doesn't need me anymore. She's got Martin.' I know that sounded like the behaviour of a spoilt child, but I was in no mood to be even-hearted at that point.

Mr Curtis talked me into deferring rather than giving up my study. The lease on my apartment had more than a year to go so he arranged to sublease it for six months. If, at the end of that time, I was still determined to spend the rest of my life in India, then he would take care of winding up the lease. He also helped me with passport, transfer of money, booking to Bombay and a decent hotel when I arrived.'

*   *   *

'Poor darling.' Veronica hugged him and gave him a chase kiss on the cheek. 'I've often thought that Fate had dealt me a foul blow, familywise, but at least I knew who my mother was and, oh yes, she was certainly there in my life. Perhaps I should visit her when we get back, just to let her know that I'm still alive. But, tell me, did you really go to India?'

'Oh yes, I went to India, and that was another lesson I had to learn. Remember I was only twenty and like most twenty-year-olds who have recently left the family home for the first time I thought I was quite sophisticated, a regular man about town. Did I have a thing or two to learn!'

'Do tell.'

CHAPTER 12

India

'As always, I had left the planning of the trip to someone else. While I sat around sulking Mr Curtis had made all the arrangements. Three weeks after my interview with him I was on my way to Bombay. This was the first plane trip I had ever taken, and it was such a long one. I spent most of my time staring out of the window at this new, white world I was hurtling through at a speed I dared not think about. There were no roads, no hills, or valleys, to mark my progress. I was in another world. I closed my mind to what was beneath me. I had never been particularly fond of the sea and the thought of a watery grave was so appalling I tried not to think about it. I clutched Amah's ashes as if someone was threatening to steal them. I even took them to the toilet with me. I had neglected my grandmother all my life and now her ashes were the most precious possession I had.

I don't remember much of the trip until they announced that we were approaching Bombay airport. Then I became alert. This was my homeland, the place of my birth. I looked expectantly out of the window as the plane came in to land. I could see people walking almost on the runway, men, women and a few children. I do not know whether they lived alongside it or were just using it as a walkway, but they seemed oblivious of the closeness of the descending plane or of their own safety. I suppose they were used to it but that first sight was the beginning of many that terrified me during the next few hours. Holding the urn in one hand I disembarked.

The first thing I became aware of was the smell. It was as if half the curry shops in London had opened their doors, and that was only in the terminal. Dazed, I followed those in front of me, got through passport with only a few questions about why I was here and for how long I expected to stay, then joined the crowds retrieving their luggage. It seemed as if life depended on grabbing it before it was stolen. There were porters everywhere and some of them looked a bit unsavoury. I couldn't understand a word they were saying. I only had one case so decided to retrieve it myself. I was jostled and pushed as I tried to reach for my case while holding the urn up in the air. It was a near thing. I had come to scatter Amah's ashes in India but not all over the floor of the arrival lounge.

Eventually I retrieved the bag and got through customs easily, thanks to the paperwork explaining the urn. Then it was out into a sauna. If it was this hot so early in the morning, I thought, what is it going to be like during the day? I was wearing a light, cotton suit and an open necked shirt but everything was sticking to me. I could feel perspiration running down my legs. I would have taken off my jacket but could not hold it along with my case and the urn.

If the terminal had smelt of curry, outside the air was thick with every conceivable human and vegetable odour overlaid by petrol fumes. If I had been a smoker, I would have been afraid to light up for fear of setting the place on fire. There were more people than I could have ever imagined, pushing, shoving, shouting, waving. I was one lost soul in a sea of humanity.

Just when I felt that I would slowly melt into this maelstrom, I spied a boy holding up a cardboard sign with my name written in large black letters. Never had my name looked so wonderful. Thanks again to Mr Curtis, not only had my accommodation been arranged, but a taxi was there to pick me up.

'Good morning, Mr Langford, my name is Zinda, and I am here to take you to your hotel.' Had he been an angel sent straight from heaven he could not have been more welcome. He pushed his way towards a waiting taxi.

And then I realised where all the petrol fumes were coming from. Every taxi was belching smoke from its exhaust as it idled, waiting for customers. In another lane people were risking life and limb trying to snare a car before someone else jumped their claim. It seemed that only when one was sitting inside a vehicle with the door closed could you be sure that you were the recognised passenger. I was beginning to realise that, without Mr Curtis' careful planning, I would have probably been trampled to death in the taxi ranks and Amah's ashes would have joined the smoke and fumes.

As we pulled out onto the road, I noticed that, even at this early hour, the road was crammed with cars, wagons, carts and animals. I could see little else as the taxi alternately sped along, came to sudden, jolting halts or became almost air born when it hit one of many potholes. I had never been a nervous passenger before but now I clenched the urn close to my chest, closed my eyes and waited for an accident. I prayed that I would be killed outright and not left maimed and bleeding by the side of the road.

The taxi came to yet another violent stop. When it did not move again, I opened my eyes to see the most imposing of buildings, as big as the houses of parliament I thought at the time.

Zinda, who was sitting beside the driver, jumped out, opened my door and, smiling broadly, ushered me out,

'We are here Mr Carter. Welcome to the Taj Mahal Hotel, the finest hotel in all India.'

I gathered my various parts together and stepped out. Now I had another difficulty, how to get my wallet out and pay the driver while holding onto the urn. I swapped it over into my left hand and extracted the wallet. Zinda and the driver looked at me expectantly. I hesitated, then, handing the urn to the boy I turned to the driver. I had a large wad of notes but had no idea of their value. I held one up. The driver scowled. I held up another. He looked doubtful. I pulled out one, more colourable that the rest. His face broke into a beaming smile, and he began nodding vigorously.

'No,' the boy shouted, shoving the urn back and taking my wallet. Then he and the driver entered into a spirited argument before coming to a satisfactory arrangement. He took the required notes and handed all but one to the driver, pocketed the other, and gave me another radiant smile

'Taxi drivers are never to be trusted. You must call on me when you wish to use one. I will see that you are not cheated.'

I assured him that I was not going anywhere at the moment, but would certainly call for him if I did. He led me up the stairs to the entrance where a magnificently uniformed doorman with a stiff, white moustache gave me a military salute.

The raj still rules here, I thought.

The street had been noisy and smelly but inside peace reigned. At last I felt it safe to take my first long breath. India might be my birthplace but only here, amid surroundings I understood, did I feel safe. I realised how tired I was. All I wanted was a warm bath, and a long sleep between crisp, white sheets.

The boy led me to the reception desk, announced my arrival then held out his hand waiting for a tip. I realised that the other note had been for his help rescuing me from an unscrupulous driver. I handed him the note rejected by the driver. He looked seriously at me for a moment, then accepting it with grace, sped off, no doubt to help some new, innocent traveller.

But my troubles were not over. Because of the early arrival, my room was not ready. The desk clerk apologised over and over but it was the rule. Rooms were not vacated before ten a.m. and, to allow for cleaning could not be occupied before twelve. I assured him I understood.

'The same rules apply in England, but is there somewhere I can sit in the meantime?'

'Of course. You can have a comfortable chair in the foyer, breakfast in the breakfast room or perhaps you would like to read the latest news in the morning paper in the reading room.'

'I do not need food and have no interest in the day's news, currant or otherwise, but I would, however, appreciate a tea or coffee.'

A young man was summoned to escort me to a high backed, cane chair stuffed with cushions and beside it, a small table on which was a pot and a delicate cup and saucer. I relaxed back as the young man poured the most delicious cup of tea that I had ever tasted.

I must have dozed off as the next thing I heard was a voice with an American accent

'Careful there pardner, you'll have that drink all over yourself in a minute.'

I woke with a jerk, spilling a little on my trousers, but they were already damp and stained so a little more wouldn't hurt.

'I bet I know where you've come from,' he said in a friendly tone. 'I bet you've just come off a plane and can't get into your room,'

'Yes. How did you know?'

'In the same boat. All the way from L.A. and can't get in till twelve.'

'I've just got in from London. I would kill for a bed.'

'I should be used to it, but long-distance flights get to me too. Not my wife. She sleeps all the way and is a cheery as a cricket when we land. She's off now looking for a quiet place to do her morning spiritual exercises before she greets the day.'

'Spiritual exercises? You mean like yoga or something?'

'No. These are prayers that must be said at sunrise. She does the yoga thing too. She's a followed of Meher Baba.'

'You mean the guy that Peter Townsend ...'

'Yeah, that's the one. My wife has been a Baba lover for several years. It keeps her happy. Course it nearly broke her when he died, pardon, left his mortal remains, but it hasn't dampened her fervour one bit. We came here while he was still alive so this time we are going to pay our respects, so to speak.'

'And you?'

I only believe in things I can touch or smell, but I have an open mind. It seems to work for Faye and anything that pleases her pleases me. She's the easiest wife I've ever had and I've had three. Wouldn't trade her for Miss America.'

You wouldn't believe it Veronica, but Milton was the easiest man I ever met. After five minutes I felt as if I had known him all my life. And Faye was just the same, a little bit dippy and inclined to break into prayer or exaltation at times, but friendly. In no time I was telling them my life's story.

'And that's your grandmother's ashes in that there urn honey?' she inquired. 'What are you going to do with them? Scatter them in the Ganges?'

'No. Amah was not a Hindu. She was a Christian so I'm going to find some spiritual place associated with her.'

'You could come with us to Meherabad. That's where Baba is buried. It's about the most spiritual place in all the world. They have a big cemetery there.'

'No, Baby, I think it's just for believers,' Milton corrected her.

'But it would still be all right to scatter her ashes there I'm sure. She sounds such a nice lady. I'm sure she would have believed in Baba if she had met him.'

'No, Faye,' I protested, 'Amah was a Catholic. I'm sure she would want it to be something to do with the church.'

'Where are her people buried?' Milton asked.

'I have no idea. Her daughter and my father are buried somewhere in America. I don't want to offend, but I'm sure she wouldn't want to go there.'

'No offence taken. I'm sure she wouldn't want to be buried among strangers.'

'And her husband was killed somewhere in Malaya, during the war and no one knows where he was buried. I know nothing about her Indian family.

'My dear young man you must realise that is only her mortal remains you have in there. Her spirit has been set free. But I can tell she needs to be settled. If you are so inclined I could pray for guidance for you as you meditate. That way she will be able to contact you and give you guidance.'

'Now Faye,' Milton interrupted, 'this young man might not want Baba's help.'

But she was so sincere I did not want to offend her. I told her to go ahead. I closed my eyes and tried to think of a place where Amah would be happy, while Faye began a soft chant. I couldn't understand most of it but I heard Baba's name mentioned a number of times. At last she stopped chanting and I opened my eyes.

'Well, did anything come to you?' Faye asked expectantly. 'Did you see some special place or hear some special music or anything like that? Sometimes it isn't clear and you have to talk it over a bit.'

'I'm sorry to disappoint you,' I apologised, 'but the only place that came to mind was Beechwood.'

Faye's eyes lit up. 'Where's that?' She was sure I had got a message.

'Oh, it's a place in England. It was where I grew up.'

'And your Grandma lived there too?'

'Yes, until Minty moved.'

Fay's face became really serious for the first time since I had met her, 'Young man, how could you say you have not been given a message when it's clear as day that your dear old granny wants to rest in the place where she was so happy?'

'But why should I believe she was happy there. I didn't even know she was my grandmother then. I treated her like a servant.'

'Of course she was happy. She loved you. She could see you and care for you. She could watch you grow up.'

'But England isn't India. She was a stranger there.'

'And you think she isn't a stranger here? I think you should look deep into yourself, young man.'

'Now, now, Faye,' Milton chided gently, 'leave the boy alone.'

But Faye would not be stopped. Baba had given her guidance, and she would follow his prompting. 'Why have you really brought these ashes back to India, to please your grandmother or to appease your own guilt? You say you neglected her in life. Well, isn't bringing her ashes here the same thing. No matter where her ashes lie, will you ever visit them? Are you not abandoned her again?'

The shock I felt must have been visible to Milton. 'Now, that is hardly fair, Faye.'

But I held up my hand. Her words had really struck home. Why had I embarked on this crusade? Now that Faye had forced me to look at it I could see that I was only doing it for self-satisfaction; to say to that selfish grandfather of mine that I was more generous than he, that I was not bigoted like him. I was not doing this for Amah, I was doing it to spite him, and I didn't even know him or if he would even care.

'I think she's right, Milton. I think I've gone about this half-cocked. It seems I have flown half way round the world just to satisfy my own ego.'

He didn't know what to say but Faye was radiant. 'Thank you, Baba,' she prayed. 'Thank you for speaking directly to this misguided soul and showing him the way. Blessed be your holy name.'

Then she smiled at me. 'Baba has whispered to me that you must join us at the ashram and pray for peace in your soul. You are feeling bewildered now. You don't know what to do but Baba will show you the way. He will cast a light on your darkness and give you a purpose to your life.'

*   *   *

'And did you go?'

'Oh yes, I went. I had the most amazing month. I lived in rather primitive conditions and the food was nothing to write home about, but I met some amazing people and had experiences I had never dreamed of.'

'Were you converted?' Veronica asked, a little anxiously.

'No, if you mean, did I become a devotee, but I took on board quite a bit of his philosophy, if that is what you could call it. There were a number of sayings, advice, predictions that could be interpreted any way you wanted to, but basically it was all about peace and harmony, doing good, things like that. But I couldn't have coped without Milton. He didn't take any of it seriously, but he didn't mock it either. His theory was that if something works for you, go for it.

I did do a lot of soul searching and realised that I was not Indian at heart. My rejection of my upbringing was nothing more than a childish attempt to thumb my nose at my grandfather for what he had done all those years ago. Minty had said that he was just a product of his time just as Indians are today. She was right. We are all the same really, if you care to look.'

Veronica was completely absorbed in the story. 'So, what final happened to Amah's ashes?'

'I brought them back to England. Took a lot of explaining to customs that time, but Indians have great respect for the dead, unlike English customs officers, and I got them home. They are now on a little plinth in the garden she loved. I will always keep Beechwood so I can visit her every time I go down. I'll take you there and show you, if we ever get off this island.'

'That would be nice. Now, after all this storytelling I'm ready for bed.' She snuggled up and they lay close. There was nothing sexy about it. It was like cuddling your best friend.

Veronica was soon asleep, but Carter was restless. The conversation had focused his mind back to his time in India. It was easy to say that he went to India and then came home but it hadn't been that easy. It had been the time he finally grew up and came to accept his strange beginnings.

*   *   *

Once he had come to terms with the facts of his birth and the rejection of his family, he experienced something like a rebirth. He spent his time in the ashram pondering existence. If he wasn't the person he had believed himself to be for all these years, then who was he, really, and where did he belong? He took his dilemma to Milton.

'All my life I have considered myself English to the core. I grew up on Agincourt and Waterloo, Nelson and Drake. I was as English as the ancient oaks that grew in the New Forest. I had never thought about the concept of loving ones country. I was English, therefore I loved her. Now I have discovered I am half Indian, that my roots go just as far, perhaps even further back in India. Shouldn't I have some feelings for that country too?'

'But I feel nothing. I thought I would feel a great surge of love for my new country, the place where I was born. But there is nothing. No, that's not true. I feel revulsion. India is too hot, too dirty and there are way too many people. What is wrong with me?'

'I hear you, Carter. I hear you,' Milton said. 'But what have you seen of this country? Bombay airport and this ashram, apart from the view from the taxi window on our way to Meherabad. I'm going a bit stir crazy here too, but Faye is having such a good time I'd hate to say, time to go home. But if I suggest to her that you need a bit of salvation by getting to know your Indian side, I think she would give me her blessing to take you on a journey to meet yourself.'

'Would you really? Would you do that for me?'

He smiled. 'Course I would. I'd be doing both of us a favour. And another thing, why don't you leave Grandma at the ashram to keep Faye company while we are gone. It would mean a lot to her.'

Carter had still been carrying the urn around with him. It sat on a little shelf in his room, and he always took it with him when he left the ashram. It was as if he believed that by caring for her ashes, he was apologising to Amah for his former neglect of her when she was alive. Milton believed he was giving the boy a chance to unload his feeling of guilt.

'All we need now is a reliable driver,' he said.

'Well, I can help there. I know just the person to ask about that,' Carter told him. 'For a reasonable price he will arrange it all for us.'

I contacted Zinda who found us an honest driver with a reliable car but, 'to make sure you are not swindled along the way I myself will accompany you,' thus providing himself with a holiday from his usual business of taking care of new arrivals.

A few mornings later, Faye stood at the ashram's gates, holding Amah's ashes, chanting blessings and waving them goodbye.

They spent the next month crisscrossing India from Devprayag Junction, where the Ganges begins, to Calcutta and the Delta, where it flows into the Bay of Bengal. They saw everything, from obscene wealth to abject poverty, magnificent palaces to filthy slums. They visited temples, mosques, cathedrals, shops, markets and stalls. They witnessed joyous celebrations and burial ceremonies. Zinda had planned an itinerary equal to any that a travel agency could offer, and he filled their days with gossip and information that the ordinary traveller could never hope to come by. Carter so enjoyed his company that he gave him a bonus over and above that which he had requested.

But the journey itself had not been a success. Apart from Zinda, nothing or nobody had moved him. Though he marvelled at the buildings, was repulsed by the poverty and amazed at the survival skills of these millions of people, nothing had touched his heart. All he felt was a tourist's curiosity. He spoke to men and women from all strata of society, listened to them discuss politics, world events, philosophy and commerce but found the only topic he could engage in with enthusiasm was cricket.

The one thing that did lift his spirits was Milton's company. In his mind he saw them like father and son. He could pretend that Milton, who was close to his father's age, was taking his son on a holiday to show him his beloved India,

He began to realise that he had never had a father figure in his life. Minty was the closest thing he had had to a mother and Charlie could possibly have fulfilled the role of grandmother but there was no substitute father. Mr Curtis had been there for advice and one or two of his teachers had kept an eye on him, but no one had touched his life as a father would. Now Milton seemed to be filling that void.

The night before they were to return to Meherabad, Milton asked, 'Well, Carter, do you feel a little more Indian now?'

'Unfortunately, I don't. It is full of wonder and the people are amazing the way they work so hard to rise above the tide of poverty, but I still don't feel I belong here. I thought I would feel some love, some pride inside me but I feel nothing but an outsider's curiosity. Is that wrong of me?'

'Not at all, young man.' Milton gave him a reassuring pat on the arm. 'As I see it Carter, though your grandmother was Indian, your mother was half English, so really you are three parts English and only one part Indian. All your memories are of England, so you are hardly rejecting a place that had so little to do with your life. India, to you, is your Grandmother, and though you neglected her when you did not know, I can see that you love her now. So, cherish her memory and you will be loving the part of you that is India.'

They parted a few days later at the airport, Milton and Faye to their home in Los Angeles and Carter to London, promising to keep in touch. He was anticipating a new, deeper appreciation he would now have for the country to which he felt he belonged.

He was looking forward to the euphoria he would feel as he

walked through the tunnel into the airport. He took a deep breath of English air and felt... nothing.

Well, it's only the airport. Perhaps it will feel different when I am in London itself, he thought. But again, nothing. He liked the familiarity and order, but where was the faster beating heart, the tear smarting at the corner of the eye, the sudden lifting of spirits?

He was home. That was good. But he wanted more than *good*.

The tenancy on his apartment had still some time to run so he booked himself into a hotel and spent several days visiting friends, going to night clubs, walking in Hyde Park and along the banks of the Thames, but though it was comfortable to be back among his own, he still wanted more.

He picked up his car and decided to drive to Beechwood. As he headed south, along the M3, it was as if a band, which had been restricting him from the time he had first learned about Amah, was loosening. He could breathe easier. He looked at the urn, sitting on the seat beside him and smiled.

'It's OK, Amah. I'm taking you home, home to Beechwood where you will be at peace and will always be there to greet me no matter how far I roam.

CHAPTER 13

A Hidden Room

When Carter woke next morning Veronica, already dressed, was pottering around in the kitchen.

'Don't get up. I'll cook this morning.'

'I do breakfasts,' Carter told her. 'You've spoilt my little surprise. I was going to bring you breakfast in bed.'

'I don't like eating in bed. It gets too messy. But don't let me spoil your little surprise. I'll shower and dress while you play mother.'

He decided to impress her with his banana pancakes, which she duly complimented. They took their coffee onto the veranda, sat on the cane armchairs and watched the little, white capped waves roll lazily onto the sand.

Watching the tides come and go had become one of Carter's regular habits. It controlled the order of his day. At low tide the reef was covered by a thin layer of shiny grey blue, like some huge mirror, as flat as a billiard table, except where erect corals formed a barrier, around which little eddies disturbed the tranquillity. This was the time to look for shells and tiny tropical fish.

Almost unperceivably the water would come back and long rolling waves, fringed with white, would return and the grey reef disappeared under the swell of rising and falling blue water, the sea coming back to claim the land. This was the time to swim, snorkel and spear fish.

Now that food might become a priority he would have to hone

his hunting skills. Couldn't have Veronica outdoing him.

'The tide is coming in. It will be deep enough to go swimming in an hour or so.'

'Pity there's no real surf,' Veronica said. 'I could impress you with my surfing.'

'The only time you'd get surf beyond the reef would be if there were a hurricane.

'Do they have hurricanes here?' Veronica sounded a little anxious.

'I assume they do but it's not hurricane season so we're safe.'

They gazed idly at the silver blue sea, comfortable in each other's company.

A sudden thought came to mind. He was here to get away from Ponce, yet Veronica seemed to know him. Was she part of the same conspiracy to entrap him?

'Veronica, how did you come to know Ponce?'

'Through Reggie, of course. He was one of the clients for a time. He sometimes needed the services of a beautiful woman on his arm when he went to important dinners and things. I have been his escort a couple of times. He goes mainly to meet and mingle so you have to entertain yourself once your there.'

Carter felt a twinge of jealous but tried not to show it. "You haven't ...' He didn't know how to finish his question.

'That is most improper of you to ask, Carter, but seeing we might be spending the rest of our lives as castaways I will satisfy your curiosity. The answer is a resounding no. I don't think any of the girls have. Some of them believe he's gay but personally I think his sperm is so important that he doesn't want to waste it on anyone less that a Lord's daughter. Someone worthy of his inheritance. Actually, he's not very stable. He sees himself as Fitzwilliam Darcy but he's more like William Collins.'

Carter laughed. 'That is a pretty good analogy, Veronica. He might be waiting a long time to be called Sir.'

'Why. His father is one, isn't he?'

'His father has always thought that he was the nearest relative to a title, but it seems maybe he's not.'

'Then who is?'

'Who knows? It could even be me,' He laughed at the look of surprise. 'My dear, you may possibly be sitting beside a genuine Lord.'

'Why only possible?'

He didn't know how to explain the strange idea that had been growing in his mind. His father had been disowned by his father. Perhaps the man he had grown to hate was, in fact, Lord James Alyward. It would answer a lot of questions. It would certainly explain the strange goings on of the last month or so.

'I'm afraid it is another long story, but it can wait. That wonderful breakfast has so invigorated me that I want to do something. Swimming's out for the moment so use your well-trained entertainment skills to think of something.'

'We could explore the interior of the island. So far, apart from the putting green, we haven't gone beyond the beach.'

'I think little else has been cleared, except for that. Golfing seems to be the only extra activity provided, and since all this rain it will be overgrown too. I could get out that "push me, pull you", lawn mower and clean it up. Then you can show me up at putting too.'

'I thought you told me that your ambition was to be captain for England?'

'Yes, but only at cricket. If you really want to explore, I suppose we could head into the interior, but I don't fancy climbing up and down hills, cutting my way through vines and creepers full of snakes and spiders.'

Veronica shuddered. 'Are there really snakes here?'

'Wouldn't have a clue but aren't jungles full of them?'

'OK. Let's skip the jungle. But there must be something here but beach. How about that little cottage. Who lives there?'

'That belongs to the caretaker, but he seems to have taken a holiday too.'

'Then what's in that run down shed?'

'That, my lady, is the most important building on the island. It contains the D.C. plant.

'A dc. plant? I've never heard of one of those. Let's go and look at it.' Veronica was already up and heading towards the stairs.

'It's not an exotic plant,' he informed her. 'It's a machine which, if the gas runs out, will provide us with basic electricity. The agent gave me a quick rundown on how to get it running, but I already know all about them.' He followed her outside. 'I know I'm a genius with machinery but perhaps I should introduce myself to it before we actually need to use it.'

The old, wooden shed was not very large and seemed to be full of man things and empty boxes. While Carter took the tarpaulin off the machine and began inspecting it Veronica wandered around, picking up pieces of metal and bits of wood. She decided to inspect the boxes. Her eye was taken by a piece of a dusty carpet,

'Carter, look at this. I reckon it is a rather good Persian rug. What's something like this doing in a dirty old shed?'

She grabbed one end and tried to lift it but found it had been nailed to the floor.

'Carter, look. It's covering a trap door. Leave that stupid machine and come and help me open it. There might be treasure down there.'

'You've been reading too many adventure books,' but he stopped what he was doing and leant his muscle to the task.

When they had pushed back the boxes and managed to raise the trapdoor, they gazed down the hole and, in the gloom, they could see what looked like a long room with cupboards, bunks and a small table.

'Is it an air raid shelter?' Veronica suggested.

'No. I think it's a hurricane shelter. It's a place of safety until the worst is over. It looks pretty well equipped. Grab that torch on the bench and we'll go down and inspect it.'

They spent some time inspecting the underground room. There were three cupboards marked, survival food, first aid and survival gear. There were also six large bottles of mineral water and a high-power battery lamp. There were even several books.

'Someone could survive down here for several days,' Carter said.

'Do hurricanes last that long?'

'No, but it sometimes takes time for help to arrive.'

'Like three weeks?' Suddenly the adventure didn't sound such fun.

'Don't worry, Veronica. Trevor will have sent someone to rescue us long before we have to use these.' But he was beginning to lose faith in his friend.

He pointed the torch towards the end of the room. 'Look Veronica, there's a door at the end. There must be another room.'

But when they opened it, there was nothing but a dark passage.

'See, I told you it was all about pirates.' Veronica said triumphantly.

They were eager to explore. After a short distance the timber lined walls gave way to rock and the path, which had become little more than an uneven track, seemed to slope upward, eventually ending with a ladder.

'Now this is what I call an adventure,' Veronica commented. 'Why didn't we sus this out sooner? We've been sitting around all day doing nothing. This is as good as Disneyland. I bet the island is teeming with secrets, skeletons and buried treasure. It would make the perfect pirate hideout.'

Carter shone the torch upward and saw the sky. 'Sorry to dampen your imagination but I think this is just an escape route should the trap door be blocked by falling debris.

They climbed up the ladder onto a rocky clearing in the jungle, facing towards the sea.

'They've really thought of everything. You could signal for help from here if it was impossible to reach the beach.'

'We could set up a lookout and signal passing ships' Veronica suggested.

'We might have to,' Carter agreed. He meant it in jest, but that niggling feeling was back. What if Trevor had betrayed him?

It wasn't long before they tired of sitting on a rock looking at the view. The lookout had been well positioned. They could see the airstrip in one direction and the other way gave a clear view of the house, the caretaker's cottage, the beach, the lagoon and over the bar to the open sea.

'Carter, the pancakes were delicious but not all that filling. All this adventuring has made me hungry.'

'Me to.'

'Let's make a survival meal from the supplies in the cupboard.'

'I think not. I hope we will never have to use them but if a message from Trever doesn't turn up soon we might be needing them for real.'

'Trevor again. Carter, you have got to tell me everything about this friend of yours who seems to hold our future in his hands.'

'OK. But let's go back to the house. I really am hungry, and no storyteller does his best on an empty stomach.'

They took their plates and glasses onto the balcony, not just to enjoy the view but to take advantage of a pleasant breeze that had sprung up.

'OK. Storytime.'

'Soon as I finish,' Carter promised. 'Where did I leave off?'

'With you deserting your good friend for good times and political activists.'

'We were certainly political, but I wouldn't say we were very active, except with our mouths. We believed we knew what was wrong with the country, but we weren't committed enough to let it interfere with our comfortable lives. What a pompous prig I was. But back to Trevor. It all started with a letter from Mr Curtis.

Dear Carter,

I have not seen you for some time, but I have been following your progress. I think I have already congratulated you on your final results. I feel some pride as I would like to believe that I played some small part in your upbringing. I hear, on the grape vine that you are doing credit to us at Woodwood and Sykes, but I am still waiting for the announcement of that "special bridge."

Enough of the small talk. This is really a business letter. I'm afraid I have reached the time of life when I must retire. I have built the old business into a worthwhile practise but, alas I leave no heir to inherit. I should have encouraged you to study law. Then I could have left it to you.

I have finally completed negotiations and the business is to be sold. I believe I have chosen well. Garret Kirkwood comes highly recommended. He is an old Kings man, but much before your time. I would like you, in the next few days, to make an appointment with regards to your estate. If it is your wish, Kirkwood will continue managing it, but you must meet him first and decide for yourself. If you are agreeable, and I hope you are, then all it needs is a signature or two from you and things will go on as usual. If there are any changes to be made, now would be a good time to do them.

'The letter made me think what a self-centred person I had become. I had learnt nothing from Amah's death. Once again, I was getting on with my own life, ignoring those who had made it possible. I remember the good Father Keenan saying, "You're a good soul, Carter, but you have a lot to learn about people." He was right.'

'I think you are being too hard on yourself, Carter.'

'Thanks, but remember, you have only known me for a few weeks. Anyway, the upshot of the letter was a visit to Curtis and Co. and, if the letter was a reality check, that visit was a real wake up. The first person I saw when I walked in was Trevor. I vaguely remembered hearing that he had passed his finals, but now that my visits to Beechwood were mainly for r & r I had not had much contact with the locals. I didn't even know that he had been working for Mr Curtis for some time.

We greeted each other like long lost brothers, which in a way we were, and arranged to meet that evening. Then I went into Mr Curtis' office, met Kirkwood, liked the look of him and signed the necessary papers. My affairs had been handed over from Curtis and Co. to Kirkwood and Partners.

After that Trevor and I met regularly, at least once a month, in the city or at Beechwood, if our visits coincided. He is engaged to a local girl and goes back every chance he can. Claire is a lovely girl. I envy him.

The next two years passed without incident. At Woodwood and Sykes, over the years, I had had some input into several large government contracts. I enjoyed the work but in the recesses of my mind I was disappointed that none of them had involved building bridges.

I had a joined a cricket club and was regarded as a success, but I had no ambition to devote my time or energy to developing my talents. Cricket had been reduced to a game, not a life.

My circle of friends still contained a couple of ex-King Alfred boys but most times I socialised with friends I had made at Queens or through cricket. At least once a month I would spend the weekend at Beechwood, walking, reading and entertaining old friends.

It was on one such weekend, as I was idly reading through the Times that an article in the obituary columns caught my eye.

'Lord Alyward's dead,' I remarked to one of my city friends, who had joined me for the weekend. 'He was a friend of my mentor, Mervin Curtis. His Lordship came to visit me once at school.'

My thoughts turned to Ponce. 'A very obnoxious relative of his made my life a misery for a time there. I suppose now he will, at last, be a real Honourable.

'It says here that they made their money from sugar in the early 1700s and Lord Alyward himself served, with distinction in India, and during the war. I remember that, even though he was quite old, he was ramrod straight. I almost saluted him. Regular Raj, I'd say. I doubt he'd have approved of Ponce.'

I would have forgotten about the article if it had not been for a conversation I had with Trevor about a month later.

'Carter, did you ever hear of someone called Sir James Alyward?'

I had an image of the very upright, elderly gentleman who had once visited Beechwood.

'Yes, he was a friend of Mr Curtis, I think. In fact, he visited me once when I was young and was most impressed when I told him I was going to captain the English cricket team. I really believed it at the time. What ambitions we had then.'

'Yes, didn't we? I was going to be the next Pelle, even though we didn't even play soccer at St Cuthberts. But, back to my question, something strange happened at work last week. Sir Alyward died recently and, a couple of weeks after the funeral, Ponce and his father came to the office. They were cloistered with Kirkwood for some time and the meeting did not seem to be a happy one judging from the raised voices. Mr Kirkwood rang through asking me to bring a certain file into his room.

'Just as I opened the door, I heard Ponce exploding, 'Carter Langford? Little Tar? What's he got to do with the old boy?' Then Kirkwood noticed me, and everything went silent. He reached out for the folder then dismissed me. I don't think Ponce even recognised me.'

'So?'

'Those files along with everything related to the Alyward account have been in Kirkwood's office ever since, so I have no idea what they have to do with you, but whatever is in them seems to have got the great Ponce quite agitated.'

'Sorry, I can't help you there. I'm none the wiser than you. Apart from the connection with Mr Curtis I know nothing about the man. Perhaps he remembered my ambition and left me something in his will and Ponce is disputing it. His father is Sir Alyward's heir, you know. Perhaps there is not as much money in the will as they thought.'

'I was only mildly interested in Trevor's story and would probably have forgotten it had not a few strange things happened to me shortly afterwards.'

Veronica waved her finger. 'Ha, the plot thickens. Don't tell me you are in a battle with Ponce over his inheritance?"

'I still don't know but there have been too many coincidences. There is something there and it has to be more than a few hundred pounds. My theory, and it is just only a theory, could be the result of an overactive imagination, but if I'm right, then it would explain a lot.'

'And what is your theory?'

'That Sir James is my grandfather. Pour me another drink and I'll present my evidence. Then you can give me your verdict. Am I a legitimate Lord or am I a deluded idiot?'

As she waltzed to the cabinet, Veronica laughed. 'And here I was, bemoaning the lack of a T.V. This story gets better than any reality show and I'm part of it.'

They settled back, drinks in hand and, Carter continued.

'This is where the story starts to get murky. The first incident happened at Xaviors. I had arranged to meet a couple of friends there. I had not long entered and was just standing, looking around, trying to see my mates on the floor or at one of the tables, when I felt someone touch my pocket. You don't expect that sort of thing in a place like Xaviors, and anyway I had nothing valuable on me, but instinctively I reached down and found the end of a gold chain hanging from it. Either the thief was an amateur or it is harder to put something into a pocket than to take it out.

I turned around just in time to see a chap, in a dark suit, hurrying towards the door. As he reached it, he seemed to give a nod to someone in the room. I followed his look and saw a young woman, seated at a table near the small bandstand, nod in acknowledgement and begin to rise.

I already had had the words "stop" in my throat, but I changed it from "stop thief" to "stop the music." I roared it as loudly as any West Ham supporter and, clutching the necklace in my fist, I held my arm aloft and charged towards the bandstand, keeping my eye on the woman all the time.

She stood, statue like, her hand clutching her throat, like an actress suddenly struck with stage fright just before her entrance. She was way out of her depth.

My interruption had a dramatic effect. The sounds of music, talking, tinkling of glass, fell like confetti. Soon there was complete silence. I pushed my way to the grandstand, still holding up my arm. I had the attention of the whole room. I didn't need to shout.

"Sorry to interrupt, but has anyone lost a necklace?"

I had given the girl her cue. She grabbed it and ran with it.

"My necklace, my necklace," she called hysterically. "My *necklace is gone.* It belonged to my grandmother. It's gone."

She was good, I'll give her that. Once I had given her the line, she was back on track. 'Then Madam, I think this belongs to you. You should take better care of the family heirlooms.'

I stepped down from the stage and walked towards her. I could see fear in her eyes, but I had decided to play it cool. Perhaps she was genuine after all. She was gushing with her thanks and apologies, but I brushed them off and turned towards my friends who were converging on me with applause, congratulations and free drinks. I tried to forget my suspicions and had a great night.

In the light of day, my suspicions all seemed a bit ridiculous. I couldn't think of a single enemy I had who would pull a trick like that. There definitely had been the dark suited chap who had deliberately put the necklace in my pocket, but was it just coincidence that he had chosen me? Perhaps he had dumped it in the nearest pocket because he thought he had been sprung. Perhaps the girl really was genuine? The more I played these thoughts over, the sillier they sounded. In the end I dismissed them, but it had made me wary. That is probably why I was alert when the next incident happened.

'Again, it was at night. I had been at the Royal to see *Chorus Line* but, because I was heading down to Beechwood the next morning, I declined an invitation to party on. For some reason I had trouble getting my key into the car door. When I did get in I noticed that the light in the glove box was on. It had a funny catch and sometimes did not switch off. I was about to push it shut when some instinct said *check first*.

Lying on top of my service manual was a plastic packet containing white powder. I leant over to examine it but, as I straightened up, I saw, in my rear vision mirror, a black car pulling into a park nearby. My instinct said, *set up again*. I pulled out just as the other car stopped. As Dury Lane is close to Russell St I headed straight for it. Better to make a fool of myself than get caught with drugs. The black car pulled out again and followed me until I was almost at the station then, probably guessing what I was going to do, sped off.

I took the package to the front desk and explained how it had come into my possession. The sergeant on duty listened to my story, said it was probably a hoax, but he would have the contents examined straight away.'

CHAPTER 14

Trevor's Plan

'And was it a set-up?' Veronica asked.

'Don't know for certain,' Carter replied. 'But I got a polite letter a few days later thanking me for my diligence and civic mindedness but no mention of what the packet contained. I have heard nothing since. I still didn't know if I was becoming paranoid or if I had an enemy out to get me.

'I needed to talk it over with someone I could trust. I thought about taking my problem to Minty and Martin then, remembering my conversation with Trevor, told my tale to him instead.

'I know it all sounds like an episode from The Avengers, Trevor, but you have got to admit it is pretty weird.'

'I agree. Leave it with me and be super careful in the meantime.'

A week later he rang and insisted that we meet that very night. When I arrived, he was waiting and seemed somewhat agitated. He could hardly wait for us to sit down.

'Has anything else suspicious happened?' he demanded.

'Nothing to report sir,' I joked, but he didn't appreciate the humour.

'This is not a laughing matter, Carter. Someone is out to get you.'

That sobered me up, quickly. 'Who?' I could see he wasn't joking.

'Can't name names, but you have got to take this seriously. I still hadn't been able to get my hands on the Alyward files so, after coming up with nothing at the office I paid a visit to Mr Curtis. I knew he had been your guardian and he had been good to me when I first started, and I had kept in touch. As he would have dealt with the Alyward file originally, he would have known if there was anything in them, anything that related to you. After all he had been handling your affairs since you were a child.

Once again, I had ignored old friends, I thought. Would I never learn?

'I told him all about the events in the office and the strange happenings in your life. He was immediately engaged.

"Jones," he said. "This is alarming news. Now you must listen very carefully. I'm sorry I can't give you an explanation at this point, but you must believe me. Carter is in danger. You must get him out of London immediately. Not Beechwood, somewhere where he will not be found easily. I will put my mind to it and contact you as soon as I have a place to send him. He may resist or at least want an explanation, but you must insist that he follow my instructions. I would do it myself, but I am too close to the problem, and he may be traced through me."

'I knew then that there was definitely a serious problem if Mr Curtis was worried. 'So, he is in danger.' I said. 'If someone is trying to kill him, why can't you go to the police?'

"I do not believe that murder is the objective. I can say no more, but you must tell him to be very careful until I come up with a plan, and tell him to be ready to leave at a moment's notice."

Trevor insisted that I go straight home and stay there till he contacted me.

Veronica eyes widened. 'Wow! That was a bit dramatic. And did you?'

'Of course. When the two people in the world you trust, absolutely, tell you to do something, you do it.'

'But how do I come into the story?'

'It is not a story, Veronica. It's real life, but I'm glad that you are a part of it, though I still haven't figured out how you came to be in it.'

She was indignant. 'So, you suspect me too?'

'I wondered at first, but I can't see you sharing a conspiracy with the Ponce.'

'Then it must be Trevor,' she declared, but Carter shook his head. He still had faith in his friend, but there was a niggling doubt.

'Trevor didn't organise all this, Mr Curtis did, and he is the one person in all the world I would trust with my life.'

'Then how does your Mr Curtis know Reggie?'

'Reggie?' Carter queried, 'Oh, your boss. What makes you think that Mr Curtis knows him?'

'Well, he was the customer who arranged our meeting.'

'Mr Curtis? He wouldn't know anyone like Reggie.' He shook his head. 'No that can't be right. I met you at *Maranos*. In fact, it was the receptionist who introduced us.'

'And who suggested you go there?'

'Trevor, but he was following … oh, of course, he would be following Mr Curtis' instructions.'

'That's if his story is true. Did you go and see your friend?'

'No, I obeyed orders and stayed home till Trevor contacted me.'

Veronica gave him a sad look. 'What a good, obedient little boy you are. Tell me more.'

Carter became more confused. The more he thought about it, the more suspicion seemed to fall on Trevor, but he still wasn't convinced.

'Well, whoever made the actual arrangements, Trevor was the messenger. He came to me to discuss the plan. 'How would you like to spend a week or so on an isolated island?'

'You mean in the Shetlands?'

'No, a luxury villa in the Bahamas.'

'Sounds great. I'm getting pretty tired of looking at these four walls. How long will I be there?'

'Hard to say, one week, two maybe. Shouldn't be too long.'

'Can I take a lady friend along with me?'

'I suppose company would be nice, but not someone you know. Mr Curtis thought you might ask that, so suggested an escort would probably be better.'

'Curtis? I can't believe he even knew such things exist.' I still couldn't take the whole thing seriously, but Trevor certainly did.

'I assure you he does. He has given me the address of a reputable place. You can meet the girl first, see if you like her then, if she is suitable, you can both fly off to a tropical holiday on Friday. That will give you time to cancel any appointments etc. and you can drop a hint or two that you may be paying a quick visit to America or Australia. Don't be specific. That way nobody will get suspicious when they don't see you around for a while.'

I still didn't know what was going on, but if Trevor and Mr Curtis thought it was that serious who was I to question, so I followed orders and this,' he extended his hands, 'is the result.

'And you still trust your friends?' Veronica asked.

'What else can I do?

Veronica frowned. 'Carter, I can't vouch for the loyalty of your friends, but I can shine a bit of light on your story. Reggie rang me, told me he had a nice job for me if I wanted. It would mean going away for a week or two. Venue would be "A" class and the company safe. "Come to the club tonight and look him over. Your choice luv, but you would be doing me a big favour if you agree."

'So, I was set up.'

'You could say that, but remember, you were checking me out too.'

'So, we are here by mutual agreement. I'm glad we both said yes.' Carter gave her a little hug. 'But now I'm beginning to worry that we have both been sacrificed.'

'I can't believe Reggie would sell me out.'

'I feel the same way about Trevor. But either way there is nothing we can do about it now. We will just have to go on trusting them but come up with some options in case things go pear shaped.'

They sat, each silently contemplating the strange sets of circumstances that had culminated in their presence on the island. Was it coincidence or part of some sinister plan?

Carter was not, by nature, pessimistic. His had been an unusual life. He was used to processing data, filing it in imaginary files then getting on with life. Whenever things got difficult someone always seemed to appear in his world and solve the problem for him. Had he been religious he would have said he was blessed. But this time he was on his own. Veronica hardly counted. What troubled him most was that he wasn't sure what the problem was, or even if there was a problem at all.

'Come on Carter, let's do something. Sitting around isn't helping. We've got to make a plan, we've already found a secret hidey-hole. Who knows what other secrets there are on this island'

'Like what?'

'Well, maybe we'll find a hidden boat and sail away from here.'

'Veronica, I don't know anything about boats, do you?'

'Well, I've been sailing once or twice. Anyway, it might be a motorboat.'

'And do you know exactly where we are and how to steer to

civilisation?'

'OK. Not such a good plan, but we must do something. How about I teach you how to spear fish?'

The fishing expedition was relatively successful and after doing his best to scale them, Carter fried the proceeds over an open fire. By the time they had separated the flesh from the bones the meal was hardly adequate, but Veronica did not complain. They remained on the beach as the sun slipped behind the breakers.

'The one disappointing thing about tropical sunsets is that they are over so soon,' Veronica remarked, 'and then the mozzies come out.' She stood up, brushing the sand from her legs.

'Let's stay a little longer,' Carter said, 'I'm beginning to feel comfortable here. Isn't this the life that millionaires spend their lives working towards?'

They remained on the beach until the sea was almost up to their campfire.

'That's paradise for you,' Carter said at last. 'Come on, let's go home and wait for the moon.'

'Carter, did you hear yourself? You called it "home." Are you giving upon rescue?'

'No. But it doesn't seem so important anymore.'

Chapter 15

Visitors

When they woke next morning, their anxiety seemed to have diminished. In fact, they began to discuss, positively, how they could survive and live on their tropical island. They still believed that sometime in the near future someone would come to rescue them, but in the meantime, they would enjoy the life fate had dealt them.

'We could build a large bonfire on a high point and light it if a ship or aeroplane appears,' Veronica suggested. 'And erect a banner or something on the lookout platform.'

'In the meantime, we should make an inventory of all our food stocks and plan our menus accordingly, drinks also. I think it would do us both good to cut down on our befores and afters.'

'Carter, I've just had a thought. I wasn't planning on a long stay, so I only packed a month's contraceptives. I don't want to give birth with only you here to help.'

'Then we will just have to practise restraint.'

'Just like a real, married couple.' She rather liked the idea.

After a leisurely breakfast Carter sauntered out onto the veranda and looked out beyond the expanse of lagoon towards the breakers. It would be several hours before they could go fishing but, if they wore shoes they could search the coral for molluscs. There might even be oysters. He was just about to share his thought with Veronica when he noticed a dark smudge on the horizon that turned into the shape of a ship before his eyes.

'Veronica, quick, grab those binoculars. I think a saviour is at hand.'

They watched, mesmerised, as a white cruiser came closer and anchored close to the bar. They raced down the steps, waving and shouting. By the time they reached the beach a small motorboat had been lowered and two people climbed into it.

'I hope they've got shoes on. There won't be enough water for them to land. They will have to anchor their boat and walk the rest of the way. '

They watched the boat putter along until the motor grated on the coral. One man got out and began pushing the boat closer to the beach.

Carter looked closer at the second man who seemed to have no intention of lending his weight. There was something familiar about him.

'Veronica,' he whispered, 'It's Ponce. What's he doing here?'

'It's a trap, Carter. Let's run and hide while we have a chance.' She ran up the beach, but Carter did not follow.

Whatever he is here for, he doesn't know that I suspect him, Carter reasoned. I'll play dumb until I get some idea of what he's up to. They won't be able to leave for a few hours yet and I know the island better that they do.

He waded out to meet his visitors. 'Ponce, 'pon my soul. What are you doing here?' and began to lend a hand to push the boat in as far as it was possible.

'Is there someone else on the island with you?' was Ponce's response.

So, he doesn't know about Veronica, Carter noted. It will be interesting when he finds out who she is. 'Oh yes, I have a delightful little companion. You must come and meet her. I'm afraid you will have to get your feet wet, Ponce. Your boat has run aground. Give me the anchor and I'll run it up the beach. That will keep it secure till the tide comes in. You won't be able to go anywhere till then.'

Ponce took off his shoes, rolled up his trouser legs and stepped gingerly into the water. The boat rocked and he would have fallen had Carter not held his arm. He had been tempted to let him fall, but felt it helped his image to appear to be so trusting. It seemed that Ponce was in the dark about a lot of things and Carter was going do all he could to keep him there.

He hurried up the beach towards the steps before Ponce had time to speak. He wanted to reassure Veronica. He knew that Ponce had not recognised her. That would be another surprise.

'Darling,' he called. 'Open the bubbly. We have guests.'

'What are you doing, Carter?'

'Don't worry. He's already way out of his comfort zone. He'll really flip when he sees you.'

Ponce was thoroughly uncomfortable by the time he reached the veranda. The bottom of his trousers were wet and his feet were cut and covered with sand. Carter indicated a cane chair.

'Thanks, Tar. Sorry to drop in on you this way.'

'Don't mention it. We have visitors dropping in all the time, though most of them wait till high tide.'

Ponce frowned. 'So, other people know you're here?'

'Of course. We're a regular watering hole for sailors.'

Veronica made her entrance carrying a tray with bubbling champagne and handed each man a glass. Ponce turned to accept a glass and nearly dropped it.

'Veronica! What are you doing here?'

She was back in character. 'My dear Ponce, no gentleman would ever ask a lady such a question.' She shook her head, and he lowered his eyes.

'Sorry,' he mumbled, grabbed the glass and swallowed half of it in one gulp. Of course, the bubbles caused him to cough and splutter champagne everywhere. He apologised profusely as Veronica handed him a large napkin and refilled his glass.

Carter was really enjoying his confusion. It also confirmed, in his mind, that Ponce did not know very much about what they were doing here on the island. As Veronica handed him his drink she winked. *She's up to something too,* he guessed.

When both visitors had been served, she sat on the edge of Carters chair.

'Oh, Carter and I are old friends,' she informed the visitors. 'When he invited me to join him, how could I refuse? I know this island well.'

'You do?' Ponce almost spilt his wine again.

'Oh, yes I have been here several times with Lord... er... a distinguished older gentleman.

The little minx, Carter thought. Mention of a Lord has really rattled him. I've suspected that this island belonged to the late Lord James. Now I'm sure of it.

'But how did you know I was here?' Carter asked.

Things were not going the way Ponce had planned them. 'Um... Your friend Jones told me.'

'Trevor? But how would he know I was here?'

'Oh, I don't know. Perhaps it was Kirkwood, someone from the office anyway.'

'Kirkwood? Oh, I remember. He's the new owner of Carter and Co. I went to see him when he first took over. He would have handled the bookings and things I suppose. I'm hopeless when it comes to things like that. I just mentioned to Mr Carter that I needed a break, and he arranged it all.' He took a sip from his wine. 'Veronica, fill up their glasses. They are almost empty.'

She did as she was commanded. Ponce's friend, who had taken no part in the conversation had already drained his glass and Ponce was so confused that he drained his and held it out for another. He tried to continue the conversation but found it hard to concentrate.

'Do you have staff?' he enquired.

Carter was still thinking about how he would answer that question, but Veronica was way ahead of him.

'No, the caretaker has frightened them away.'

'The caretaker?'

'Yes. He's the weirdest person I ever met. He just comes and goes.'

'Veronica, that's not fair.' Carter wasn't sure what she was up to but was willing to go along with it.

'But he is spooky, Carter. The way he just suddenly appears beside you. One minute you are alone and then there he is, almost standing in your shoes. I reckon he's into voodoo or something. He gives me the creeps. Let's hope he doesn't materialize while you are here, Ponce. If he takes a dislike to you, you have to watch your step.'

Carter could see that Ponce was trying desperately to concentrate but whatever Veronica had done to the drinks was having its effect. The other man was already slumped in his chair.

'Where... where ish he?' Ponce was already slurring, and his eyes were closing.

'Manuel? Who knows, 'Veronica shrugged. 'He's supposed to live in that little house over there on the edge of the jungle, but he could just appear on the veranda any minute.'

Ponce gave one terrified look towards the veranda then

succumbed to the sedative Veronica had added to the drink.

'God, Veronica, what did you lace the drinks with?'

'They are pretty strong sleeping tablets. I hope I haven't overdosed them.'

'Well serves them right. At least you have given us time to make a real plan.'

'Let's take the boat and get right the way out of this.'

'No,' Carter reasoned. 'First, the tide is out, two they have a ship blocking our exit and three, we don't know how to navigate, remember.'

'So, are we just going to sit here and wait till they wake up?'

'Hardly. We don't know why Ponce is here, but I bet it isn't to rescue us. No, we'll just go to ground and wait for them to make the first move. First, we will add to our food and water rations, then we will make it so uncomfortable they'll go.'

'So, you think they'll leave?'

'Sooner or later, or perhaps when help arrives.'

They busied themselves for some time, choosing some nibbles to take in case it was a long siege, hid most of the rest in a cupboard under the stairs and took off all the fly screens. Flies would be a nuisance during the day but after sunset battalions of mosquitoes came out. There would be no rest inside for the two sleeping men.

'They must be beginning to wonder what is going on,' Veronica said, looking towards the cruiser.

'If they are half the sailors they should be, they will realise that there is no way of getting back until the lagoon is deeper. They probably think we are having a reunion. Unless they too are part of a plot.'

'Well, they're in for a surprise when no one turns up.'

Carter took one last look around before they left.

'Seems a pity to just leave them sitting here,' Veronica said. 'Couldn't we tie them up or something?'

'No, that would give the game away, but I've got a better idea. What was all that about the caretaker?'

'I was just trying to scare him.'

'Well, let's scare him some more. Ponce seems so dead to the world that I think we could move him without him waking.'

'Move to where?'

'To the cottage, of course. When he wakes, he won't know where he is and when his mate wakes, he will think Ponce has deserted him.'

'Great. Let's really do his head in, strip him of his Saville Row jacket and dress him up in that revolting Hawaiian shirt you bought. And some beach shorts. That will really freak him out.'

When they had redressed the sleeping man he was wheeled to the cottage in a wheelbarrow and seated in a chair facing the jungle. It would be the first thing he would see when he woke.

'And I'm going to take his clothes and hide them. Just imagine how demoralising that will be for him, wandering around like a beach bum.'

By noon, Veronica and Carter were rearranging the shelter in case they were in for a long stay. Then they went up to the lookout to see how things were going on in the outside world. There was still no activity from the house.

'That was some powerful sedative you gave them. I hope they're alright.'

'One usually knocks me out for about five hours, so two couldn't have done too much damage, but look, Carter, isn't that the motorboat bobbing around in the water?'

'So it is. The sand must have become soft as the water came back. Now we're all stuck here unless they have a lifeboat or something.'

They laughed, but Carter didn't know if it was actually to their advantage. It would mean that Ponce and his companion could not make a quick retreat. They were both in for a long wait.

CHAPTER 16

Where's Veronica?

If sitting around on the island had been boring, sitting in the shelter was downright purgatory. They went up periodically to the lookout but nothing seemed to be happening either on the island or on the ship. Back in their hiding place Veronica entertained herself rearranging the cupboards yet again, planning the meals they could make from their stocks and planning different ways to get them out of their predicament. She even began going through Ponce's pockets to see how much money he had on him.

'Look, Carter.' She held up a plastic bottle containing little white pills. 'They're sleeping pills. I think they were meant for you. I'm so glad I got in first.'

'So, he was going to drug me. I wonder what he had planned for me afterwards?' He contemplated his fate for a time. Suddenly he had an idea.

'How much longer before they wake, would you say?'

'At least another hour, maybe two. Why?'

'I think I've got an idea. That chap who was with Ponce will be just as confused when he wakes up. He will have no idea where Ponce is. I reckon I can play with his mind too. If I woke him up, he would be rather confused. I could take advantage of that.'

'What do you mean?'

'Just you stay down here, or go and watch things unfold from the lookout but, on no condition come out.'

'Why?'

'I'm going to wake him, then play it as it comes.'

'Carter, be careful.'

'I will be, but promise me, don't come out. I've seen too many movies where the whole plan gets messed up because the little woman has to follow the hero.'

'OK hero. I'll stay away and watch you save the world.'

He gave her a quick kiss, then opened the trap door. He noted that the wind had picked up. Weather's changing, he thought. Probably start raining again.

When Carter got back to the house nothing had changed. The room looked more or less as it had before. Ponce's friend was still sleeping peacefully in his chair. Carter sat watching him for a time, developing the plan he had formed. When he had rehearsed it over in his mind and could find no flaws, he decided to put it into action. Feeling he had nothing to lose he stood up and started shaking the other man, shouting, 'Wake up! Wake up!'

As soon as the man responded, Carter stood over him and demanded 'What have you done with Veronica?'

'Veronica? What?' He was still feeling the effects of the sleeping pills but tried to concentrate. *Someone was shaking him and shouting like a maniac.*

'Don't try to fool me,' Carter shouted. 'I never sleep in the daytime. I've been drugged. I suppose you were supposed to be watching me. Well mate, you've fallen down on the job. So, tell me, what have you done with Veronica?'

Ponce's friend was coming out of his bewilderment. 'Who's Veronica?'

'Don't play the innocent with me. You know who she is. It was clever of Ponce to pretend he didn't know she was here. What's he want her for? If he hurts one hair on her head I'll hunt him to the end of the earth.' He was playing his part so well that the other man became frightened.

'Take it easy, mate. That wasn't the plan at all. He was supposed to drug you and take you back to the boat.'

'What? Drug me? Why? What would Ponce want with me?'

'Look, I haven't got a clue. I was hired for the muscle in case you resisted. Where's Ponce?'

Carter put on what he thought would be an expression of sudden revelation.

'If you're telling the truth, then I suspect he's run out on both of us. When I woke up here you were out to the world. I reckon he spiked your drink too. I've looked everywhere but can't find either of them. He's gone, and Veronica's gone too.'

He advanced towards the man again and shook his fist in his face. "What has he done with her?'

'Hey! Back up man. Whatever this Ponce, as you call him, was planning, it had nothing to do with me. He hired us in Miami. Said it would be a quick trip. Just had to pick up a spy or something. Said he didn't expect any trouble, but brought me along, just in case.'

'And you bought that shit?'

'I know it sounds a bit odd now but at the time it sounded OK. He's very plausible that friend of yours. Kind of implied he was with the secret service or something. Said he was a lord or something. Showed us his passport, Honorable Ponsemby Neighsmith. That's what it said.'

'Oh, yes, he's claimed that title all his life, though it is debatable whether he is.'

The man laughed. 'I think Ponce suits him better. Anyway, we took him at his word, and the money was good.'

Carter walked towards the veranda. 'Look,' he shouted. 'The boat's gone. He's taken her back to the ship and left you here. You're lying. What were you supposed to do with me?'

But the other wasn't listening. As soon as Carter mentioned the boat he ran down the stairs shouting, 'Neighsmith! Neighsmith! Where the hell are you?'

He raced into the water until it was deep enough then began swimming towards the boat which was still bobbing around in the waves which now had white caps. He was a good swimmer and he struck out strongly until he reached it. He climbed aboard and after a couple of attempts got the motor started and headed back towards the ship.

Carter decided it was time for him to disappear again. He noticed faint footprints that he had left behind earlier so, breaking off a large palm branch, he walked backwards to the shed using the palm to cover his tracks. He didn't think Ponce would notice but was not taking chances. The wind was strengthening so, with any luck, all traces would be blown away.

There were a number of empty cardboard boxes in the shed, so he decided to stack them haphazardly around the trap door. He then opened it and, standing on the steps, reached out and pulled a few of them onto the lid as he lowered it. Again, he rather doubted whether Ponce, if he came into the shed, would notice the rug but, with boxes on top he would probably miss it altogether.

He had hardly reached the bottom step when Veronica, who had been watching from the lookout, appeared from the other end.

'Carter, what did you do? That chap headed into the water like a channel swimmer.'

'He's gone looking for Ponce. I convinced him that Ponce had drugged us both and ran off with you.'

'What do you think he'll do when we are not on the ship?'

'Who knows, but at least we have only Ponce to deal with. Has he come out yet?'

'There was no action from the cottage when I last looked but I was so engrossed watching you and that other guy. He should be waking up soon. I would love to be there when that happens.'

Veronica laughed at the image her mind had created.

'Better to let him think he's all alone on the island. Just think. He wakes up in a strange house, can't find anyone and has to wander around in someone else's clothes. Let's get back to the lookout and see what he does.'

They were both in a happy mood. They were in a safe place and had a ringside seat to goings on on the beach.

There was no movement from the cottage for some time, then a head appeared around the open door, followed by the rest of a suspicious Ponce. The wind was almost gale force, the palms blowing wildly, and the first drops of rain were making splashings into the sand. He looked tentatively all around then raced towards the house as if expecting to be intercepted at any moment.

'I wish there was a surveillance camera or something in the house. I'd love to see his face when there is nobody there,' Veronica said.

'That will be nothing to what he will do when he realises that the boat is gone too.' He trained the binoculars on the cruiser. 'Look at the ship! They have pulled up the anchor. They must be heading out to sea for safety. I wonder how long this storm will last.' Carter laughed. 'I almost feel sorry for him.'

The mention of a storm worried Veronica. 'Is there going to be a hurricane?'

'No, this is probably only a tropical storm, but they can be pretty rough too.'

Veronica grabbed his arm and pointed. 'Look, he's running down to the beach. Surely he's not going to try swimming away.'

They watched as the drenched scarecrow fell on his knees on the sand, howling to the elements, then staggered back, pushing against the wind and rain, to the shelter of the house.

'Veronica, I think we should retreat too. This lookout doesn't feel all that safe.'

They headed back to the safety of the bunker and, for the next few hours entertained themselves talking, playing a few hands of canasta and preparing a meal. From their sanctuary they had no idea how fierce the storm was but, realising that it would be dark outside, settled down for a night underground.

'I wonder how Ponce is going, all alone up there?' Veronica said.

'God knows. But I would hazard a guess that he has tried to seek oblivion with a bottle of whiskey.'

They had their first meal of survival food, which, because of its novelty, they thought quite good, but neither wanted to live on it for long. 'If they hang around for more than two days, I'll be ready to surrender,' Carter said.

Conversation topics dried up. Their minds were on other things. Veronica suggested they get an early night so they would be fit for whatever tomorrow held, but lying on their bunk beds, their minds drifted back to the comfortable king-sized bed in the house and then wandered from room to room wondering what was happening up there.

They both woke early, breakfasted on a couple of health bars then went up to the look-out to see what, if anything, had changed since yesterday.

'If that was just a storm I wouldn't want to be here in a real hurricane,' Veronica observed, looking at the debris strewn along the beach.

'That's nothing, just nature's way of getting rid of the rubbish. In a real hurricane all those trees would be flattened,' Carter assured her.

'Have you been in a hurricane?' Veronica asked with some awe.

'No. But I've seen lots of them on telly.' He saw her look of disappointment, so turned his attention towards the sea. 'The cruiser is not back yet. I wonder how long it will be before they come to rescue Ponce.'

She looked back to the house. 'And I wonder how the poor fool is.' She had a thought. 'Carter, what would happen if he wasn't there when they came back?'

'Now there's an interesting scenario. Do you think we could spirit him away? We could bring him down here?'

'No, I've got a better idea. Let's scare him so much that he begs to be taken off the island.' She had a mischievous gleam in her eye.'

'Veronica, what are you planning?'

'Not sure yet but, will you let me handle this one? Don't interfere unless I call for help.'

'OK, if you're certain.'

They went back to the shelter and Veronica climbed the steps to the trapdoor, pushed the boxes aside and walked towards the house. Carter went up with her but waited in the shed.

Veronica had no idea what she would find inside, but even her wildest imaginings would not have prepared her for what she found.

Ponce was sprawled across the couch, dead to the world and dressed in nothing but a pink, silk negligee of which she was particularly proud.

Where had he found that, she wondered, then remembered that it would probably have been hanging on a hook in the main bathroom.

She looked in there and found the sodden garments he had been wearing, lying on the floor along with a large towel. She guessed that he had staggered into the bathroom, removed his clothes, possibly showered, then, having dried himself grabbed the nearest thing to cover himself before seeking oblivion with drink.

She had a brain wave. Why not continue the Manuel fantasy? She shook him gently but there was no response. Good, she thought. He's out to it for some time yet, long enough for me to paint the scene.

She went first to the servant's quarters and, as she hoped, found a maid's black dress and white apron. Whoever owned this place, they certainly pulled out all the stops when entertaining, she thought. She would have liked to have found a waitress' cap, but made do by tying her hair on top of her head and winding one of her scarves around it. Then she opened her vanity case and covered her face with brown mascara.

'Well, it's hardly convincing,' she told her mirror image, 'but in his befuddled state it might work. Anyway, here goes. If it all goes pear-shaped, I will have to call in the cavalry.'

'Oh Master, Sir,' she began in what she imagined would sound like a West Indian voice. 'Wake up please, sir. You're in the wrong room.' She shook him vigorously, and in time there was a reaction.

'Come quick, Master. You are in the wrong house. Emanuel will be very angry. He will harm you if he finds you here.'

The name rang a bell in Ponce's befuddled mind.

'Manuel?'

'Yes, Manuel, the Caretaker. He does get so cross if guests don't sleep in their own room. Hurry, please Sir,' and she dragged him to his feet. 'This way, Sir.'

His confused mind registered three things, a maid, the wrong room and Manuel. That name put fear into his blood. He tried to co-operate.

He was conscious of being led out of the house then blacked out again.

Carter, who had been watching, sprinted across the sand to help Veronica as she half carried him towards the caretaker's cottage. 'What are you doing?'

'Don't ask questions. I'll explain later. Just help me get him inside.'

Carter could hardly contain his mirth at Veronica's strange appearance as they half dragged, half carried Ponce to the cottage, sat him comfortably on the same chair as the one he was in earlier, facing towards the jungle, then retreated.

'He'll be out to it for some time yet,' Carter observed. 'So you'll have plenty of time to explain the plan and the costume.'

'Don't you recognize a West Indian lady when you see one?' She twirled around. 'I was only trying to plant an impression in his mind. If I was successful, he will think that some maid found him before Manuel and rescued him.'

'Manuel? Oh, the caretaker. Where did you get that name from?'

'Don't laugh. I think it was Manuel in Faulty Towers.'

'But he's Spanish and wouldn't scare anyone.'

'I know, but whenever I think of a non-English waiter it is always

Manuel. It wasn't too much of a stretch to make him a caretaker.'

'Well, he certainly drew a reaction from Ponce. Hope he remembers when he wakes up. And now tell me, why is he dressed in your negligee?'

'You'll have to ask Ponce himself. My guess is that it was the first thing he could find. Now, unless you feel a sudden attraction to my new persona, I would like to return to my usual boring self.'

They went back to the house and, while Veronica showered and dressed, Carter went to the storeroom and selected a few tins and packets and well as a frozen Chicken Mornay Supreme. He hoped they wouldn't need them but at least they had more appeal than the survival food in the shelter.

'Do we have to leave, Carter?'

'Just to be on the safe side, until we are sure the cruiser is not coming back and, even though I don't think we'll need it I'm going to take a spear gun. If we do get discovered, we will at least be able to defend ourselves.'

'Oh, Carter you do inspire one so. I can just imagine you at the entrance of the look-out defending us like some medieval knight but instead of a sword you will have a spear gun.'

They re-entered the shelter laughing at the image.

CHAPTER 17

Gone Up In Smoke

Sometime after they had returned to their observation post the cruiser appeared on the horizon. They watched as figures on the ship surveyed the beach, waved their hands around making decisions then, having come to a decision, launched the small motorboat.

'They're coming back,' Carter said. 'The tide is in so they'll have plenty of water to get right up to the beach.'

When the boat reached the high tide mark two men jumped out.

'God, Veronica, they've got guns. They really mean business this time. The guy who was with Ponce looks really mad.'

'With Ponce or with you?'

'Not sure, but I'm glad I'm not in his sights.'

They watched as the boat was securely anchored, then, leaving the other on guard, the one who had arrived with Ponce the first time, rifle at the ready, began to survey the beach, then the house. Having met with no opposition he clambered up the stairs, shouting, "Neighsmith, Neighsmith, show yourself.'

He must have satisfied himself that the house was empty for he soon appeared on the veranda, fired a shot into the air, then headed for the cottage, again shouting for Ponce.

All the noise must have reached Ponce through his alcoholic daze. He came running out, the negligee flying behind him. His sudden appearance unnerved the gunman who fired a bullet that hit the sand dangerously close to Ponce.

He collapsed onto the sand, held up his arms in surrender and cried, 'Don't shoot. Don't shoot.'

The man grabbed him by the arm and dragged him to his feet. He shook him, interrogated him and getting no sense, dragged him across the sand and threw him at the feet of the guard, obviously giving the man instructions to keep him there. He began searching the area, disappeared inside the shed but soon reappeared. Their retreat had not been discovered. Then he raced up the paths leading to the air strip and the putting green.

Eventually he must have given up the search for he went back to the beach to interrogate Ponce again but, though he had sobered up by this time, he could not give a satisfactory account of where the other two were. Instead, he kept pointing to the cottage and shouting.

'I think he's blaming Manuel,' Veronica whispered.

The man pushed him away, walked back to the cottage and then, frustrated, took out a cigarette lighter and began setting fire to anything he could find. Soon the cottage was in flames.

He stood back, a satisfied look on his face then walked towards the house. It was mainly constructed of timber and as Carter and Veronica watched in horror from their lookout, proceeded to fire it too.

He stood, hands on hips and laughed. He may not have known what the mission had all been about but he felt that, somehow, he had been made a fool of. He was not used to being bested and knew how to play hard ball. At least he now had the satisfaction of revenge.

He waited long enough to make sure that the house was well alight then walked back to the boat and almost threw Ponce into it.

140

The other two climbed in and, as soon as they were in deep enough water, started the motor and headed back to the cruiser. When they were halfway across the lagoon there was a giant explosion and bright flames reached into the air, turning everything orange.

'There go the gas bottles,' Carter said. There was nothing they could do but watch as the little motorboat powered on towards the ship. It pulled alongside and they watched as Ponce, still clad in nothing but Veronica's negligee, was unceremoniously hauled aboard.

'Oh my God, Carter, what do we do now?' She started back to the stairs. 'If we hurry we may be able to save something.'

'No. It might be a trick.'

'A trick, but they're sailing away?'

'And someone has still got his binoculars on the beach. It might be a trap. Ponce may have been fooled, but that other chap knows that we couldn't have been spirited away. He probably expects us to rush down to put out the fire. Once they know, for sure, that we are still here he'll come back. Sorry, love, but we can't surface until we are sure they have left.'

They watched until the ship disappeared over the horizon as another tropical shower fell. It was too little to save the burning building but stopped the fire from spreading.

They climbed down to the passage and back to the shelter.

'At least we will have a good meal tonight,' Carter said, pointing to the mornay.

They spent the evening talking and playing board games but there was no heart in the games and the conversation was dull. They were each waiting for the morning.

At first light they climbed to the lookout again. Carter looked through his binoculars and was gratified to see that his instinct had been right. The cruiser was again anchored just outside the breakwater. Once again, as soon as there was enough water in the lagoon the boat was launched. Ponce was not in it, but the other two landed, inspected the burnt out building, then walked into the jungle of palm and tamarind trees. They were away for a long time, but finally reappeared looking hot, dishevelled and obviously in a very bad mood.

They hurried back to the beach and sped back to the ship.

'Do you think they have given up?'

'Probably, but we'll give it one more day just to be on the safe side.'

So, they spent another day watching the sea and another night doing small things to pass the time till sleep came.

On the third day they surfaced hoping that their enemy had given up. It felt strange, walking on sand, full sunlight on their faces. They had only been hidden for a couple of days but already they had missed the fresh air and open sky. Veronica felt invigorated but Carter was despondent as he surveyed the ruins of the house.

'It's gone, Veronica. Everything destroyed. How are we going to survive?'

'Come on Carter, it's not that bad. We're alive, there's plenty of water and we have a shelter if it rains. We're not much worse off than we were before.'

'Not much worse? How can you say that? We had food, power, comfortable beds, cooling fans. I was worried before that we might be marooned on this ghastly place for a while, but at least it would be a comfortable wait. And what's it all for, anyway?'

'Only you know the answer to that.'

'No, I don't. I have some hazy idea about an inheritance but no facts and, if what I think is true and this is all about a title, I don't want it. If it is so important to Ponce that he would kill for it then he can have it? Nobody has consulted me. I've just been dumped here.'

Veronica gave him a disappointed look. 'Carter, stop behaving like a kid who's had his lollies pinched. It's not that bad. We've got food for a few days. I'm sure there is enough around the island to stop us from starving and I'm sure you know enough to make things work again. We've still got the D.C. plant.'

'And what is the use of that? All the electrics were in the house. I'm just sick of the whole thing.'

He stomped down to the water's edge and sat, staring out to sea as if he hoped deliverance would come from there.

Veronica followed him but stood, looking down at him as he indulged himself in his misery.

'Carter Langford, you are a disappointment. Didn't you tell me you are descended from a long line of fighting men? Do you think they would give up over a setback like this?'

He was about to reply that they fought from an advantage of privilege, that they probable just stood on a hill and directed operations, but then he thought of the letter his father had written. His grandfather had died in the jungles of Malaya. That wouldn't have been a picnic.

He also remembered what his father has said about the conditions in which he had found Amah and his mother. His wonderful Amah had not given up. She had not only survived but had contrived to give her daughter an education. Then she had left all the world she knew to care for him.

He might have the blood of the Alywards in his veins, but he also had hers. If she could carry on in spite of adversity, then didn't he owe it to her to do the same? He closed his eyes and tried to picture her, that little, dark woman. He remembered how light she had been when he held her. She had even defied death to give him one last chance to know her.

'Amah,' he whispered, 'if there is such a thing as an afterlife and if you can hear me give me some of your strength, your tenacity. Help me to be worthy of you.'

He sat a while longer gazing out to sea and felt a calmness, a will to go on. He became ashamed of himself for being such a coward. What was a little thing like a house, a few luxuries, against life?

'Sorry, Veronica, I did spit the dummy for a bit, but I'm fine now. The problem is that, whenever anything important has happened in my life there has always been someone, usually Mr Curtis to iron out all the wrinkles. I'm nearly thirty and I have never made an important decision by myself. Even in India there was Mervin. And now here you are to bring me to my senses. You're right, all we've lost are the trimmings. We've got all this,' he waved his hands in the air 'and we've got each other.'

He looked at her with new respect. She was caught up in his problems. It should be she who was berating him, not the other way around.

'Here I am going on about my misfortune when you should be the one complaining. You are in the same boat but have no reason to be here.'

'That's OK, Carter, we all have our moments and, though this is by far the strangest appointment I have ever had, it couldn't have been with a nicer fella and I wouldn't have missed it for the world. I only hope I live to tell the tale.'

They walked back to what had been the house, now a charred mess of burnt timber and steel piping. Because the recent rains had soaked into the timbers, a few sections of the house still remained, but everything was ruined. The large refrigerator, once gleaming white, now a smoky grey, was still intact, but the aluminium trimmings had welded the lid to the body. The metal poles which had held up the veranda now stood, sentinel like, waiting for their burden.

The cottage had not been so lucky. It had been reduced to a pile of ash.

'It really is "Me Tarzan, You Jane" this time Veronica. We're back to the primitive now I'm afraid.'

Veronica laughed. 'Just think, if we survive, I can write a book about our adventures and sell it to the tabloids. It might even become a best seller. Wouldn't that be one in the eye for the Ponce?'

"Veronica, you're amazing and I once thought of you as a feather-brained good time girl. I am so, so glad that you agreed to come on this trip with me and, no matter how it turns out, it will be worth it all just to have known you.'

Veronica, overcome with emotion, replied 'Shucks, you say the dandiest things.'

After this moment of emotion they set about planning their new life without modern luxuries.

Carter took control. 'First we must make a list of our assets, then work out how we can compensate for what is missing.'

Veronica looked towards the two large tanks which, being made of metal and standing away from the house, had not been damaged. 'We've got plenty of the most important thing, water,' Veronica said, 'even the emergency supply in the shelter.'

'Ah, yes, water. Seeing most of our food is dehydrated we will need lots of that.'

'You have spent a very sheltered life, Carter. The food may not be Savoy but there are a few luxuries.'

'Like the chocolate bars?'

'I'll have to ration myself with those or I might lose my figure.'

'Your figure can be the least of your worries here. There's no competition.'

They both laughed then Carter continued, 'Shelter, no worry, though I think I will use the veranda posts to build something up here. I don't fancy going underground every time I want a rest. Getting back to food. There seems to be abundant fish. You must teach me how to spear them. And then there are shellfish. Do you think they're all edible?

'We'll find out by trial and error I suppose. Don't forget the fruits in the jungle.'

'Well, food supplies get a tick. What about first aid? I wonder what is in the shelter.'

'I'll check later but, talking of medicines, I'm afraid my pills went up in smoke.'

'I shouldn't worry, there is sure to be some pills to make life a little easier in there.'

'They were contraceptive pills, silly.'

Carter gave her a quizzical look, then as the penny dropped he said, 'Oh, I see,' and Veronica nodded, 'Yes.'

He quickly changed the conversation. 'We seem to be OK food and shelter wise. What else?'

'Clothes,' Veronica answered immediately, indicating the blue t-shirt and red shorts she had been wearing for the last three days. 'I wish I'd known we were going to be down there for so long. I would have brought a change of clothes. I've been wearing these for three days. They are really on the nose.'

'Well, until you learn how to make grass skirts they will have to do. But you can always do what Eve did before she ate that apple. That's what I plan to do, at least while I give these a wash.'

Carter began discarding the shirt and jeans he was wearing but Veronica hesitated. It was not the idea of nudity that caused her hesitation. She had often walked around her flat naked, when alone. She had certainly disrobed before a man before, but that was as a precursor to something else. Now she would be disrobing as if nudity was another dress she would be putting on, and clothes had been so much a part of her personality. Who would she be without them?

Carter took her hesitation for modesty. 'Come on Veronica, stop playing the blushing bride. It's not as if I haven't seen you in the altogether before, and I know you have nothing to be coy about.'

That broke the spell. There was no one here to impress. There was only Carter, and he would accept her dressed or naked. She stripped and, gathering his clothes as well, went looking for something in which to wash them.

When they were dry, first Veronica and then Carter redressed, she out of a strange feeling of modesty and Carter out of convenience. He had not learnt to protect his private parts from grass and sand.

Veronica looked at her reddening skin. 'I hope there's plenty of sunscreen in those first aid kits,'

'We'll have to inspect them more closely. I was only interested in the food before,' Carter answered.

They decided to take a rest from their salvaging, go down to the shelter for a cuppa and check what other treasures the emergency kits might contain. Veronica spread out the contents of the first aid kit, bandages, sterile dressing, adhesive tape, antibiotic cream, alcohol, burn cream and aspirin. There were several tubes of sunscreen.

'At least I won't finish up with freckles on my nose,' she joked.

Carter was pleased to find fishing hooks, lures, leads and gillnets. 'We may have fish for dinner, yet. Look, a Swiss Army knife with all the trimmings and, even better...' he held up a large coil of strong rope. 'I will be able to make a proper shelter up top. We've got plenty of wood and a jungle full of palm leaves, but I was worried how I was going to hold them together. Now I'll be able to build you a neat little shelter where you can while away the hours watching the tides go in and out.'

'Are you implying that I am going to lie on the beach and watch you have all the fun?'

They were now back in their happy mood, planning their immediate future. Neither of them spoke of the nagging fear of being abandoned. They spent the next couple of hours salvaging the most suitable planks to begin the shelter and Carter laid them out where he intended to erect them. Before he had planned to just dig them into the ground but, with the rope he could lash them together and tether them to the veranda posts. That way they would be strong enough for the usual breezes. If another storm came there was not much he could do.

He was pleased with his effort and then went inland to collect palm branches which he wove in and out to make a roof. It did not have the elegance of the thatched roofs of his youth, but it would serve the purpose and he had an endless supply of material to repair it.

Veronica had helped for a time but, already sore from the sun, begged to go back to the shelter to slather herself with more sunscreen.

The boxes in the shed gave her an idea. She hurried down the steps, took the floral print cover off her bed and, using scissors from the first aid kit, cut a circular shape. She took this, a box of the adhesive tape and a large knife up to the shed, broke up a box and used one side to cut out a large spherical shape with a smaller circle inside. She taped the cloth circle over the hole and created a sun hat. It was not Philip Treacy, but it would do. She was very proud of it and offered to make one for Carter.

By the end of the day the shelter was complete. It looked like a very rough bus shelter, but it would serve the purpose for which it was built.

They were loath to leave the light so sat in their structure, watching the sun until it slid below the horizon, then lingered until the moon, almost full, began to turn the blue-black water to silver. They were creatures of the earth, the hurricane shelter had little appeal, but at last hunger drove them underground to eat a meal of nuts and dried fruit, washed down with packet soup.

'I swear, tomorrow, I will catch fish,' Carter promised, 'light a fire and eat it on the beach.'

And the next day he did. While the tide was out they collected shellfish that abounded in the shallows, crushed them for bait, then, as the water returned, he began fishing from the beach. Carter had done a little fly fishing in his youth but knew nothing about ocean fishing so cast out as far as he could and then gently pulled in his line.

He was unsuccessful for a time but eventually he managed to hook a few fish. They were quite small but gave him great encouragement. Eventually one larger one, bent on suicide, impaled itself on the hook.

Carter had never experienced such a sense of achievement. He performed a little celebratory dance in the sand then set about repeating his success. He had very mixed results, but in time had caught three good sized fish, enough for a decent meal.

While Carter was busy fishing Veronica decided to take an inventory of the edible fruits growing on the island. She proudly displayed the result of her foraging.

'Look, Carter, banana, mango and coconut, and look, a lime. I wish I had looked sooner. A slice of lime makes all the difference to gin.'

'If it hadn't all gone in the fire I would have tried one,' Carter replied, trying to join in the light-hearted banter. Then he held up the strangest thing he had ever seen. Surely they couldn't eat something like that? 'What's this?'

"This" was hard, green and pear shaped but had a thick, rough skin. 'Is it edible?'

'That my dear uneducated friend is called, by ignorant folk, an avocado pear, but it is no relation. It is actually from the berry family, but it has one large seed in the middle. The flesh looks a bit like solid custard. It is not sweet or sour, more bland but, with a bit of salt, olive oil and vinegar it is delicious.'

"And where pray, madam, did you come by such culinary knowledge?'

'Carter, I told you Reggie provided an excellent education. It's not my fault if yours has been purely Anglo-Saxon.'

'Then, I am willing to be educated, but apart from salt, and there's plenty of that around, I'm afraid the other ingredients are missing.'

'Lime juice will do as well. But we can't eat this for a few days. It softens after picking.'

'That will be something to look forward to, I hope.'

While Veronica lit a fire Carter looked for something to cook his fish in. There was a frying pan in the shelter, but he wanted to cook this meal without the help of modern equipment.

What would the original habitants have used, he asked himself? The obvious thing was palm leaves, but would they burn before the fish was cooked? He thought he had heard of burying food in hot rocks so came up with the idea of making a parcel with leaves and burying it in the coals.

They experimented with the smallest of the fish with limited success, but it was edible. They left the next two in the coals for a little longer and were rewarded with two delicious fish. The scales could be peeled off and the flesh came away from the bone, making it easier to eat off their palm leaf plates, their first "hunter-gather" meal. Both agreed that it was the most delicious fish they had ever eaten.

That night they went to bed more confident of their future than they had been for a day or so. Even if no one came to rescue them, they would survive. That was enough for now.

Afterwards they were amazed at how quickly they had adjusted to their new world, time determined by the sun and moon, activities controlled by the tides.

Veronica, looking at the desecrated bedspread, saw raw material. Why not turn it into a dress? Using surgical scissors and sutures she fashioned a primitive mu-mu. Now she had an all over covering as well as a sun hat. She had a wardrobe, even if it only consisted of one change. She would have clean clothes every day.

They had plenty of time on their hands. The only essential work they had to do was to find enough food to supplement their survival supplies but they were not bored, as before. True, the weather was on their side but finding things to do became part of the adventure.

They had sadly neglected the golf course once the rain started so it had become overgrown. Carter got out the hand mower and cut the grass. They began a daily competition. At first Carter was the star but Veronica, determined to become competitive, practised all day and soon became a worthy opponent.

Carter inspected all the rusty tools in the shed and with diligence and inspiration soon had a device for every need.

Sitting in their bush shelter, sharing pre-dinner drinks of fresh coconut milk, watching the sinking sun, Carter said. 'Do you realise we have the lifestyle that men spend their whole lives striving for. What does a millionaire do when he had made his millions? He buys himself an island paradise and spends the rest of his life fishing, golfing and lying in the sun.'

'Right, but there is one thing missing, a Xerox machine or a private, long distance phone line so that he can keep a check on the competition.'

'Surely they have to let it all go sometime?'

'Yeah, ten seconds before the last screw on their coffin is tightened.'

They told each other business jokes for a while, then Veronica became serious. 'Carter, if this is all there is, if no one comes, will we still be as happy as we are now?'

'Who knows, but as long as we stay healthy, and no natural disaster strikes us there is no reason why not. Anyway, there is nothing we can do about it so why worry?'

He was surprised at his own words, but he knew he really meant them. When life was reduced to a live or die situation the scales were in their favour. They had more control over their lives than they ever had before. There were no stupid rules to follow, no public servants telling them how to live, no clocks to control their comings and goings. They could turn night into day if they wished, eat when and where they wished, go naked without feeling shame or offending the tender feelings of others. They had what most men spent their lives working for. Freedom.

That night they went to bed, more confident of their future than they had been for some time. Even if no one came they would survive. That was enough for now.

CHAPTER 18

Hunters and Gatherers

They still slept underground, as the mosquitoes were fierce at night, but spent their days swimming, fishing, gathering food and improving their living conditions. Carter had constructed a shower and Veronica enjoyed washing the salt from her body. She now wore her hair in a single plait which she undid each day to wash out the salt and sand. Her hair felt as silky as before and she laughed, remembering the expensive shampoos and conditioners she used to regard as essential. She was now comfortable with her nudity but still wore her mu-mu and cardboard hat as protection from the sun.

Carter's skin was now several shades darker than it had been when they arrived, and he had already given up shaving before the fire happened. The hairs on his chin were already past the stubble stage. It was promising to turn into a luxurious, black beard. I think I'd pass for a Packi anywhere these days, he thought, remembering that long ago day and Minty's attempt to cover up his origins.

Minty, he thought, remembering that dear lady who was as close to him as a real mother. Would she be wondering what had become of him and would he ever see her again? A cloud of melancholy descended and for a time he lost the optimism that had sustained him. He had really neglected her of late. Would he ever get the chance to thank her for all her care?

This thought led to another. What were they thinking, at home? Were his friends beginning to wonder where he was? What if he never returned? Would they forget about him altogether or would he become a kind of legend, spoken of over a pint or two?

He imagined a conversation,

"Do you remember a lad called, Langford? Whatever happened to him?"

"Haven't heard hide nor hair of him for years. Perhaps he was killed in an accident or something."

"No. I heard he entered a monastery in Tibet."

'Cheer up, it mightn't happen.' Veronica gave his hair a pat and sat down beside him. 'You look as gloomy as a guy who lost a pound and found sixpence.'

'Sorry. I was just thinking about the world outside. Do you think they have forgotten us?'

'Would you mind?'

'Yes, I think I would. It would mean I was so unimportant that I was not worth looking for.'

'I thought you were happy here?'

'I am. But I'd hate to be forgotten, forever, I mean.'

Veronica stood and walked down to the sand and looked out towards the breakwater. She didn't want to be forgotten either, but she was beginning to like the person she had become. If they got back to civilisation, could she go back to the life she had led before? It was so superficial. Would she be willing to go back to spending her life recreating herself to suit the needs of others? She was more than a pretty picture. She wanted to be a real person, respected for who she was, not just for how she looked. She walked back to Carter who was still lost in his own thoughts.

'Carter, do you believe in God?'

'What!'

'God, you know. The old guy who runs the universe. Do you believe in Him?'

'Never thought about it much, but yes, I think I do. At least I hope there is a God. Humans are so hopeless at running things I hope there's someone out there who's got it all in hand. But I've never given it any serious thought. We used to have morning prayers at St Cuthberts and

Minty took me to church for all the important events, Christmas and the like, but that was as far as it went. When I found out that Amah was Catholic, I wondered if I had been baptised into that faith. But the only time I had anything to do with it was when she died. Old Father Keenan seemed a good sort, but I never went back to thank him for what he had done. What about you?'

'I never had anything to do with religion. My mothers' gospel was Vogue and Tatler and the great apostles were Dior and Givenchy. Heaven was the mansion that we would all live in when I married a millionaire. When Reggie took me in hand all my life was devoted to making the patrons happy. I don't think I have ever existed as a person, just an object to be admired and manipulated. This is the first time in my life that I can be me. Maybe there is a God, and all this is his way of giving me a chance at reality.'

'And am I part of the experiment?'

They both laughed, the mood lightened. 'You are such a comfort.' She snuggled up to him and they sat a long time, each comfortable in their own thoughts.

This must be what the people at Meherabad were seeking, Carter thought, detachment from worldly things, and to think we've achieved it without sitting around chanting and eating hot food. I'm living like a monk, but I have a loving companion to keep me company.

He leant over and gave her a chaste kiss on the cheek. 'I'm so, so glad that you came.'

'What brought that on?' Veronica asked in surprise.

'Nothing, but I mean it. Now, let's leave all this analysing. We're in paradise, let's enjoy it.' He stood up. 'Race you to the water,' and they raced across the sand, dived into the sparkling, blue Atlantic and frolicked like a couple of dolphins.

Veronica was secretly surprised that she adapted so well to her new role as gatherer. Granted the island was not a place where one must labour long and hard to find enough food. Rather, it had an abundance of fruits and nuts to choose from, and she was sure that with experimenting she would discover leaves and roots that would be edible also. But she was amazed at how much pleasure she got from it.

Must be the mothering instinct, she thought. She remembered an early ambition to run a tearoom, serving customers tea in little pots, along with freshly made scones with raspberry jam and cream. But that was before her mother had seen potential in her daughter's good looks and designed a very different future for her.

By the middle of the second week, what had been adventure had become routine. Carter had become such a good fisherman that the excitement was gone. They had no way of keeping food so, each day, he caught just enough fish for their daily need. There seemed to be little variety in the species, and he had exhausted ways to cook them.

'If only I had some oil or fat I could do fish and chips, that's if I had potatoes to chip.'

'Maybe that is the best thing about civilization, variety in food. What do you miss most, Carter?'

He thought for a moment. 'If a genii turned up at this moment and asked me for my order I think I would say, roast pork with plenty of crackle and apple sauce.'

'Sounds good, but if you had to eat it 3 times a day, every day, I think you'd get sick of it pretty soon.'

'I probably would. What do you miss most?'

'Right now I'm starting to fantasise about a slice of white bread covered in butter and, perhaps, strawberry jam.' This homely vision filled them both with nostalgia. After a minute or so of silence Cater sighed, 'I wonder what is going on in the outside world?'

CHAPTER 19

Meanwhile...

Poppy Cay, as the island was called, became the property of Arthur Alyward during the 18th century, to celebrate his Baronetcy. His family has made their fortune from sugar, and he felt it only appropriate that he should own his own island there. It was never permanently settled but members of the family and special friends used it as a holiday destination. In 1904, when Britannia ruled the waves and kept a motherly eye on the rest of the world, Henry Alyward, James' father, built a large establishment, in design rather like a small, luxury hotel with a separate caretaker's cottage, and installed permanent staff so that he and his cronies could retreat to it whenever the mood took them. James had taken his wife there for their honeymoon.

Raymond Miller's father had been the first caretaker and Raymond, himself, was born on the island. Polly Cay's popularity waxed and waned along with the Alyward fortunes. It proved very useful during the Second World War as a place where people from supposedly neutral countries could meet in secret to discuss world events, and at least twice a certain royal personage used it as a retreat from the stress of being Governor of The Bahamas.

By the fifties Polly Cay became a bit of a backwater. However, after independence, Lord James Alyward found it convenient to retain a presence in The Bahamas when tax laws in England were impoverishing many of the gentry at home.

Raymond had taken over his father's position but no longer lived on the island. Every three months he would spend a week there, fixing and tidying up. If the island was to be occupied by guests he would stock the pantry, employ servants, if they were required, then take up residence and clean up when the guests left. Whether there had been visitors or not, a creditable sum would appear in his bank account every three months. During all the years he had had only one crisis, when he discovered a group of hippies had taken up residence. A visit from the local constabulary soon solved that and, though there was a great deal of rubbish to clean up, little structural damage was done.

As bigger and better resorts were developed, visitors became fewer, still, he was retained and faithfully carried out his duties, with one stipulation — he needed at least one week's notice that guests were coming, as he was no longer a young man.

He had known for some time that he needed a hernia operation, but had put off the dreaded day until his wife Lenore insisted. Unfortunately, the telegram informing him to prepare the island for two guests who would be in residence for one month, came a week before this date. He was for cancelling the operation, but Lenore insisted. With their two sons in tow to do the work under his supervision, Polly Cay was prepared. Everything was completed one day before he entered hospital. His elder son, Sonny was charged with escorting the visitors to the island, seeing to their every need and to go over and check on the guests from time to time.

Though the operation was successful, Raymond's recovery was slow. It was at least six weeks before he felt well enough to resume his caretaker duties. He was annoyed when his son gave vague answers to his questions about the guests on the island and was eventually told that no one had visited the island during their stay.

'But they left, by boat, about a fortnight ago.'

'And you haven't been out to clean up?'

'I've been busy, Dad, exams are coming up soon.'

'Exams! And what about duty. Our family has been trusted with the care of da island since the beginnin' of the century. I hoped one day dat you would follow me.'

'When I get my degree I won't need to be a servant to British overlords.'

'And who do you think provided da money to give you that education?'

Raymond was furious with his son but, as no real damage had been done, he decided to leave the argument for now and contacted the company he used, to fly him out the next day.

*   *   *

When Carter had begun his working life he saw less of Minty and Martin, but he usually rang at least once a week. Just before he left for his sojourn in The Bahamas he sent a card informing them that he was going away for short holiday. Minty was surprised by the suddenness of the announcement but presumed it had been a spur of the moment decision, a romantic visit to Paris or a business engagement, perhaps. She expected he would tell her all about it on his return, or at least send her a postcard while he was away. But as days turned into weeks and then a month, she began to get worried.

'Martin, I'm worried about Carter. I haven't heard a word from him for more than a month.'

'Probably having too good a time to remember us.'

'But it's not like him. You hear about such terrible things happening to tourists these days. Martin, I don't even know where he's gone. All those planes crashing and the terrible things going on in Northern Ireland. He wouldn't have gone to Africa, would he?'

'Listen to yourself, Minty. You're clucking around like an old mother hen. He's a grown man now and quite capable of looking after himself.'

'I know Martin, but I'm worried. When I was last in London I called at his flat. Peters was there but Carter hadn't returned. Peters said that, before he left, Carter gave him three weeks off and told him not to hurry back. Taking him at his word Peters came back mid-week but he wasn't there. I told Peters that I was worried so he promised to ring me the moment Carter got back but I've heard nothing, which means that Carter still hasn't shown up. I had planned a day in London this Wednesday, so, if I haven't heard anything by then, I am going to call on Trevor to see if he knows anything. Oh, how I wish Mr Curtis hadn't retired.'

Minty was as good as her word. She called in to see Trevor at Kirkwoods. He had also become worried and agreed to meet her, after work, at a nearby coffee house.

As soon as they were seated he told her of the strange events leading up to Carter's departure.

'I thought I was being a bit paranoid but Mr Curtis took it really seriously. He made all the arrangements for the trip and told me I was not to say a word to anyone until he contacted me. Last week I began to worry, but when I rang his residence his housekeeper said he had gone to Scotland to visit a relative. She had heard nothing from him since.'

'Did she say where the relative lived?'

'No. Somewhere in Edinburgh, she thought.'

'Well, where did Carter go?'

'He flew to Nassau, in The Bahamas. He was to be met by someone there.'

'Met by someone? Who?'

'I don't know, a caretaker or something. All I know is that this has something to do with the Alyward estate. And that's another funny thing. I heard, on the grape vine, that a chap we were at King's with, whose father was expecting to inherit a title, has recently been admitted to a clinic. Nervous breakdown is the official version, but we all know it must be dipsomania. It was bound to happen sooner or later.

'The reason why I mention him is that he had just come back from a cruise in that general area. Drank himself into an alcoholic stupor while he was there, they say. May have no connection, but makes one wonder.'

'It does more than that, it makes me worried. Trevor, I'm going to go over there and see what I can find out.'

Minty was not one to rush to decisions but when she did there was no dissuading her. Martin agreed to go along for moral support and, six weeks after Carter had gone, she and Martin flew out of London, bound for Nassau.

*   *   *

As young men, Mervin Curtis and Reginal Pike had left Newcastle-on-Tyne together to find a better life away from the industrial north. Though they pursued very different careers they remained friends. Mervin did not actually approve Reggie's choice of occupation but admitted to himself that it filled a need as much as his own. Running an Escort Agency was legal, his clients came from the best of society and Reggie, himself, mixed with the rich and famous. He became a wealthy man but looked after "his girls" and most retired with a healthy bank balance.

Curtis had even availed himself of his services for some of his own clients so he had had no hesitation in recommending him to Trevor. On Curtis' recommendation, Reggie had been happy to engage Veronica as a companion for Carter on his holiday.

The terms of the agreement had been vague, three weeks to a month, so it was not until the fifth week that he began to worry about her. He would have been just as anxious for any of his girls but Veronica was a particular favourite. Already he had had to cancel two prospective engagements.

He tried to get in touch with Curtis but, when he could not be located, he remembered the young man who worked for Curtis' old firm and had organised the trip. He decided to contact Trevor and find out what was going on. It was the day after Minty had visited him, so Trevor was already looking for help in finding out what had happened to his friend. Of course, Reggie did not go in person, rather Trevor was summoned to his place of residence.

Trevor knew what a powerful man Reggie was, so held nothing back. He poured out everything he knew as well as his own suppositions. The Neighsmith name caught Reggie's interest.

'I know of the father, and also his obnoxious son. He was once a customer but has been struck off my list. I shall speak to his father.'

The next day Ponce's father received a disturbing call from Reginal Pike. At first he was annoyed, indignant, but when his son's name was

162

mention he was immediately engaged.

'Look, Mr Pike, I am as worried as you. The story is complicated, and my son is an idiot. I will try to explain. It has to do with Lord Alyward's estate. It was always assumed that I was the natural heir, but it appears that there was a grandson. It's complicated, but the upshot seems to be that I will not be a Lord after all.

'It didn't worry me all that much, but my son became obsessed with the injustice of it and vowed to regain the title. With the help of an old school friend he concocted a plan and left for the Americas. Said he was going to have a word with his rival. I was worried that he might be planning to do the boy harm, but I believe all he did was go on a cruise and spent the time turning himself into a drunken sot.

'He had to be flown back from Miami, a raving alcoholic. He seemed to have lost his mind. In the end I had to have him committed to a clinic, costing me a fortune and they are pessimistic about his rehabilitation. You'll get no sense from him. Best go to see his friend Kirkwood, of Kirkwood & Partners. Used to be Curtis and Co., gone to pot since Mervin retired I believe.'

Back to old Merv again, Reggie thought. Where is the bugger?

The next day Reggie, accompanied by a large, threatening looking man, appeared at the front desk of Kirkwood & Partners and demanded to be taken to Kirkwood's office immediately. The terrified receptionist ushered him in.

Kirkwood knew Reggie by reputation, especially his connection with many powerful men. Not a good person to get on the wrong side of and, though he didn't think he would be physically attacked in his own office, he was wary of Reggie's companion. He fervently wished he had not listened to Ponce's plea of help for the sake of "old scholar loyalty". He should never have given him a look at the conditions in the will.

So, it didn't take Reggie long to learn that Garret Kirkwood had given his friend, Ponsemby Neighsmith, details of an amount paid from Carter Langford's account for flights to Nassau and Polly Cay, and the name of a Raymond Miller, who was to be the contact person when he reached the airport.

Reggie owed his success to being discreet but thorough, and he wasn't one to leave a job half done. He would get to the bottom of this mystery and if anything had happened to Veronica, someone would pay.

CHAPTER 20

Rescue?

The first week of their new life had been exciting, in the second boredom had set in but by the beginning of the third week they had become uneasily reconciled to their fate. They had more or less decided that they had seen the last of Ponce, but were still on their guard, checking the sea around the island from their lookout each day. How they would tell between friend and foe they were not sure, but they would face that problem when it happened.

Rescue was not in their hands. One day soon, no doubt, someone would remember them and come looking for them. They would be discovered but, till then, they would make life on the island as comfortable as possible.

They had discussed the idea of building a raft of some kind but decided against it. Neither of them had any sailing experience, they had no compass and no idea in which direction the other islands lay.

They had told each other every little incident about their former lives and were beginning to run out of new things to talk about. Conversation was becoming reduced to monosyllables. They could almost read each other's thoughts. We'll be reduced to grunts soon, Carter thought as he sat, watching the same sun rise over the same horizon. Even the weather seemed to have taken a holiday, each day was picture perfect, the same as the day before. Not even a storm to break the monotony.

'You know Veronica, we really are the most useless pair of castaways. In all the stories the hero is a seaman, a cartographer or at least a friendly tribe turns up to save them.'

'And all you've got is me. But look on the bright side, it's not a desert island. There's food, water, shelter. What more do you want?'

Carter looked anew at this woman he had been spending his time with. He could hardly remember the glamorous blonde who had behaved like a pampered child when they were newly arrived. 'Veronica, you are amazing. Most women I know would be a screaming heap by now, but you? How do you manage to stay so positive?'

'Oh, I've done misery and woe, but it gets you nowhere. Remember, I'm a reconstructed failure. I could have spent my life behind a checkout. It wasn't as easy as I suggested but it was worth it.'

'Come to think of it, this adventure is changing my outlook on life too. I went through one reconstruction in India, but once home I've drifted back into my old life, a comfortable home, an easy job and money. Whether I worked or not, it was there. I did nothing to earn it except be born and I've done nothing with it except provide for my own comfort. I haven't even taken on the responsibility of a wife. I've had a few serious affairs but no commitment.'

'Come on Carter, stop beating up on yourself.'

'No, I'm serious. When, or if, we get back to civilization I am going to change.'

'Like become a missionary, or something?'

'I doubt I would go that far but I'm going to do something worthwhile with my life and I don't mean, make more money. Look what that has done to the likes of Ponce and his family. If I do inherit the Alyward fortunes I'm going to do some good with it.'

'But what will happen when you take a wife?'

'If I do, she'd have to be a lot like you—' and then a new thought came to him. Why should he settle for someone like Veronica when the real thing was right before him? He suddenly realised that she was everything he had ever dreamed of. An emotion he had never experienced before filled him with a sense of wonder. This must be what love, real love is, he thought. He had been living with it for over a month and never recognised it. He began to daydream about all the things he loved about her, her beauty of course, but her wit, her resilience, her tenderness. She was the one person he knew he could be happy with for the rest of his life.

He gave a sigh of happiness, but then a dreadful thought shattered his euphoria. He loved her but did she love him? Did she have any feelings for him at all or was he just another customer? Suddenly he didn't want them to be rescued. He wanted to keep her to himself. How could he possibly measure up against some of the men she had known? If he declared his love for her, would she believe him, would she reject him or would she just laugh at him and turn it into a joke?

He turned towards her forming a question in his mind, but she had moved. She had walked down to the water's edge and was standing, head back, one hand holding the back of her cardboard hat, looking expectantly towards the sky. He hurried down to join her. He had to know his fate. He would propose to her now, before he lost his nerve. 'Veronica,'

'Shh, Carter, can you hear something? Can you hear a plane?'

He snapped out of his pondering. 'Yes, yes, I think I can. Look out there, that speck. I think it is a plane.'

'Carter, we're rescued.' She threw her arms around him, kissed him briefly then turned back to watch the speck turn into a shape.

Carter was lost for words. His excitement was mixed with regret. Did he really want to leave this little bit of paradise, rejoin the real world? Then another thought intruded – a plane, but whose plane?

'Veronica, calm down. How do we know it is here to rescue us? It could be Ponce and his mates coming back for round two.'

'Oh Carter, no. I never thought of that. What can we do?'

'I doubt they could have seen us yet. Let's hide till they land.'

'In the shelter?'

'No, just move back into the trees. We can observe them from there. It might be a rescue plane after all. If they look like a rescue party we can run out to attract their attention. If they think the island is deserted they might fly away.'

They hurried back into the tangle of trees and shrubs and watched. The plane grew larger and larger as it flew over the water and over the beach but instead of descending towards the air strip it overflew the island altogether.

'No, no,' Veronica shouted. She sank to her knees, tears streaming down her face. She had kept all her fears to herself but now, when the possibility of rescue had been denied, she gave way to despair.

'It's all right, Veronica. See, it's not flying away, it's coming back. Come on,' and he ran out from the trees. She followed him and they both began waving frantically.

The plane came in low over the beach. They could see the pilot and another man looking down on them and pointing. They waved and shouted, ecstatic with joy. But their joy turned to despair as the plane, after almost touching down, flew back into the sky and off towards the horizon.' They were both stunned. 'Why, why, why?' Carter demanded of the disappearing aeroplane. 'The must have seen us. Why didn't they land?'

Veronica was passed giving answers or solace. She was devastated. She had had a vision of salvation. Now it had been snatched from her. She had tried so hard to be positive. She might have joked about being a castaway, tried to keep the conversation light, kept herself busy finding ways to pass the day, but she always believed, in her heart of hearts, that rescue would come. Now it had, but it had gone.

There had been several times in her life when she thought she had reached rock bottom, but this was much worse. She would spend the rest of her life until she was an old lady, wandering up and down this stupid bit of beach, looking at the same waves, filling in her days doing nothing until she died.

Carter swallowed his own disappointment and tried to console her. "It's not that bad, Veronica. At least they know we are alive. They will be back.'

But she was beyond being consoled. She walked down to the edge of the water, sank down onto the sand and refused to move. She sat for the rest of the day gazing out to sea, her back turned to the silent island. She had never felt so insignificant. She was of no more importance than the weakest of the palm trees, the smallest insect crawling up its trunk. When she died her bones would turn to dust and become nothing but grains of sand, blown by the wind, washed by the sea. And the island, which she had begun to love and trust, would remain silent, remote, unaware that she had ever walked on its beaches, swum in its sea and ate of its abundance. She was nothing.

Carter gave up trying to cheer her up and wandered aimlessly around. There was nothing to do but wait. Someone had definitely seen them. Sooner or later they would be back.

It was late afternoon before Carter heard the next noise. It was coming from the sky but it sounded different, louder but slower. He tried to rouse Veronica but she took no notice. She was beyond hope. He shaded his eyes and tried to determine where the sound was coming from. In time he saw two shapes which slowly evolved into helicopters. They hovered over the two castaways for a time and then descended, throwing up sand as they landed gently on the beach a little way away from them. Veronica did not move. It was as if they did not exist.

But Carter was galvanised. As soon as the blades had stopped rotating he ran towards them. He was brought up short as two men, in uniform and carrying sub machine guns, jumped out and advanced towards him, pointing their weapons and demanding that he get down on his knees and put his hands on his head.

He thought about protesting but seeing the official look of the men decided to comply. It was probably some silly mistake, he thought. He would explain the situation when everybody calmed down. After all, they had broken no law.

At the same time two other men were running towards Veronica. They made a similar demand. She did not respond but remained in the trance she had sunken into. While one man guarded her the other moved forward, picked up her hat and quite gently eased her up and led her towards one of the helicopters. As she reached the vehicle she seemed to come out of her trance.

'Carter, Carter, what's happening?' She tried to break away but was roughly pushed into the helicopter. The blades began to rotate then the helicopter rose and headed out to sea.

Carter jumped to his feet when she screamed, intending to run to her rescue, but was felled from behind. He sank to his knees, was handcuffed and dragged, unceremoniously, into the other vehicle.

Carter had no idea why he and Veronica had been handcuffed and forced into helicopters, or where they were being taken to, but felt a helicopter was no place to argue with armed men. Unless the men were in costume, they must represent a legal agency. They would have to land eventually. He would comply with whatever was asked of him until he could explain the situation to some proper authority.

If only he could be sure that Veronica was safe.

*   *   *

It had been Raymond Miller who had reported that primitives seemed to have taken up residence on the islands. Every building had been burnt to the ground and they had constructed a simple shelter and seemed to be living off the land. This had set off alarms in the capital. Ever since independence they had been worrying that some group or country would try to invade or start a revolution in their islands. They had an economy the relied largely on foreign investment and tourism which required a stable, peaceful government. Any suggestion of disturbance had to be nipped in the bud.

Carter knew nothing of Bahamas' politics. He only knew that they spoke English so it would be a simple matter to clear up any misunderstanding. It was not a long flight. They landed amid a flurry of sirens reporters and flashing blue lights. They were quickly hustled into waiting police cars.

Short flight, must be Nassau. Thank God, they'll speak English. Carter relaxed back into the leather seat. *Soon have this sorted out, then back to Blighty.*

CHAPTER 21

Dean Martin was still a household name in The Bahamas. Though he had not appeared in films for some time he was very popular on television. The evening Carter and Veronica arrived back in Nassau a rumour had spread that he was coming there to discuss a new movie, set in The Bahamas.

Had Dean landed that evening he would not have been welcomed by an excited press because, though they had originally come to film his arrival, they had been distracted by the imminent arrival of another kind. They had all converged on a nearby runway to investigated flashing lights and screaming sirens. They got no answers to the shouted questions but a cameraman managed to get a couple of photos as two strange people were hustled into waiting police cars.

Nobody knew who they were but that did not stop them from speculating. The morning newspaper featured a large captain, *WHO IS THIS MAN?* and underneath, a large picture of a nearly naked, hairy man.

*   *   *

Carter gave Veronica an encouraging smile as they were united at the front door and pushed towards the front desk. A uniformed officer was waiting there but gave no signs of urgency as he continued writing in a book. Eventually he looked up and sighed, 'Ah, the poachers,' then very slowly, 'do-you-speak-English?'

This was not the reception Carter had expected.

'Yes. Of course. As if you didn't know.'

His remark was ignored and the questions continued, not so loudly but still slowly. 'What-is –your – name – Sir?'

'OK. If you want to play it that way.' They had fantasized for so long about being rescued. It never went like this. Carter was seething but controlled his answer. 'My – name – is – Carter – Roger – Langford.'

The officer wrote the name on a form in front of him but, discontinuing his pronouncing game, continued, 'Nationality?'

'British.'

'And in which country in the British Commonwealth were you born?'

This question really threw Carter. No one, since that long ago event in the school yard, had ever questioned his birthright. He held out his arms to remonstrate and noticed, for the first time, how dark his tan was. Then he remembered his long hair and bushy chin.

He laughed, 'Why England, of course. But I can see how you might have made the mistake.' He relaxed ready to give the man the benefit of the doubt. Anyone could have made the same mistake.

But the man at the desk continued, 'Do you have a passport, licence, anything to identify you?'

'Come on, where would I put a passport in this?' He held out his hands indicating his tattered shorts, the only covering he had on.

The officer ignored the question. 'Do you have anything to identify you, or explain what you were doing on Polly Cay?'

'Polly Cay? Oh, the island. Is that its name? No, everything went when the house was burnt.'

'Ah, the fire, and what did you have to do with the fire Mr,' he looked at the paper in front of him, 'Mr Carter, Roger, Langford?'

The sneering way his name was spoken got to Carter. This was not a rescue operation. Something was going dreadfully wrong and now they were trying to fit him up for the fire.

'Right,' he shouted, thumping the counter, 'I've had enough of this. I am not going to answer another question until I have consular representation and a good lawyer.' He noticed that Veronica was about to be questioned. 'Don't say a word, Veronica,' he shouted, trying to reach her. 'They're trying to fit us up.'

He felt his right arm being grabbed and pushed up his back. 'Let me go.' He struggled but it was useless to resist.

The officer at the desk nodded and he was frogmarched towards the cells. 'We will speak again when you have calmed down, Mr Langford. Now Miss, if you would not mind answering a few questions?'

Carter looked back and, for the first time, saw Veronica, as she would appear to anyone who did not know their situation. They had become so used to each other's appearance that they did not see how they would look to outsiders. But now he saw a woman in a shapeless garment and crazy hat. Her hair hung down like unwound hemp and her face was dry and red with peeling nose and cracked lips. She bore no resemblance to the beautiful, young woman who had arrived on the island.

Was it any wonder that he appeared more like a wandering native than an Englishman, born and bred? What a fool he had made of himself, expecting to be treated like a civilized man. Now it would take him ages to get them to see who he really was and believe the story he had to tell. He tried to tell them that he was sorry for his earlier behaviour, that he now understood their mistake and that he would like to start again from the beginning. But his attempt was taken as further resistance and he was roughly pushed into a cell.

Veronica was not in a very stable state. The original arrival of a plane, the disappointment, the sudden arrival of men with guns, the sight of helicopters and finally the rough treatment being handed out to Carter, terrified her. It was like being in some strange, horror movie. She could feel reality slipping from her.

She was taken to an interview room and answered every question asked of her as truly as she could, but the longer the interview went the stranger her answers became. The whole story seemed so improbable that she became confused herself. The more she said the weirder the last six weeks became. How to explain why and how they got there, let alone the strange happenings afterwards. Why were they going on and on about vandalism and trespass? They seemed to be blaming them for the damage.

And what was happening to Carter? Was he being tortured? Eventually she put her head into her hands and refused to reply. The detective decided he would get no more from her so she was taken to a cell where she lay down facing the wall, curled up and tried to shut out the world.

The two people arrested did not really fit the image of criminals but they were certainly different. Perhaps they belonged to some strange sect, setting up a colony or maybe they were terrorists, intent on using the island as a launching base for an invasion. It was late in the day so, Inspector Jamison, who had been assigned the case decided to let them stay in the cells overnight then be interviewed in the morning.

He would contact Miller, bring him in to testify whether or not the two people he had in custody were the same people he had taken to the island, but when he went to see Raymond he was told that, though he had prepared the island for the visitors it was not he, but his boy, Sonny, who had escorted them there.

Sonny was angry when he was told that he would have to go to the police station next morning to identify the people. He was quite annoyed as he had plans for the next day, but knew better than to ignore a request from the police.

In fact, he was very annoyed with the whole enterprise. He had had to waste a week getting the island ready and another day taking the stupid couple there. Then he had had to put up with a roasting from his father because he hadn't bowed and scraped to them as if he were their slave. If they were in trouble, good. It was no more than they deserved.

*   *   *.

When Minty had set out to fly to Nassau she had little information to work on, only the date on which Carter and a female friend had arrived, expecting to be picked up at the airport. She did   know the name of the person who was to meet them, but not that of the island they were to be taken to. Martin had reasoned that it was very vague but she had planned to speak to anyone who had flown customers out on that day.

'If that doesn't work then I will go to the police. There must be some record of his arrival, customs or something.'

The international airport was very busy so, while Minty set about orienting herself, Martin looked at the morning newspapers at the kiosk. They were full of the account of the strange event of the day before, along with a large photo of a wild looking man, clothed only in brief shorts. Underneath, was a large caption, WHO IS THIS MAN?

Martin bought a paper, more from habit than interest, but when he looked at the black and white image he caught his breath. He shook his head. Could it be? Or was he just imagining? Without wanting to influence her, he said, casually, 'What do you think of this?'

Minty had only one thought in her mind and was annoyed when Martin pushed the paper into her hands. She gave the photo a casual glance, then gasped.

'Martin!' She grabbed his arm. 'Martin, it's him! It's him. It's Carter. Tell me I'm not imagining it? It really is him, isn't it?' She almost collapsed into his arms.

'You think it looks like him? I thought I might be letting my imagination run away with me, but if you think the same, that's enough for me. I would say our first stop should be to the police station.'

*   *   *

Carter had not enjoyed his night in police custody. The bunk was too hard, too narrow and his mind was too active for sleep. He spent the night in self-analysis, going over and over every aspect of his life. Was it his fault that he had grown up so selfish or was it just his nature? When had he ever done anything for the benefit of another? Was it his fault that he had grown up so self-absorbed?

He remembered the shock and remorse when he discovered that Amah was his grandmother, the stupid rush to India to appease his guilt. At least one good thing had come from that, meeting Milton and Faye. But he had failed to keep in contact. Why? Was he so used to others doing things for him that he couldn't keep up a friendship by simply replying to a letter? In the cold light of morning he took a good look at himself and didn't really like what he had become.

At eight o'clock next morning Carter was served breakfast but got no answers to his questions. A short time after he saw eyes looking at him through the observation hole. I'm not going to react, he thought. I'm going to behave myself. I will not let them provoke me. Time for recriminations after they realise their mistake.

A short time later Carter was escorted into an interview room. Two strange people were waiting for him. One indicated for him to sit down, then opened a folder.

'Sir, yesterday when spoken to at the desk you claimed that you were Carter, Roger, Langford. Is that correct?'

The tone sounds friendly, warm, West Indian, like Clive Lloyd. Now I will be able to explain the situation.

He didn't like the word "claimed" but decided not to make an issue of it. He nodded his head and gave a simple 'yes.'

The Inspector gave a slight nod. 'Do you still stand by that claim?'

Perhaps he should put his case more forcefully, 'I do. Look I can understand that my strange appearance could have caused you to have some doubt, but when I explain the circumstances–' but the detective interrupted.

'Then what would you say when I inform you that someone, who has seen the real Carter Langford, has made a signed statement that you were not the man, carrying that passport, that he flew to Polly Cay six weeks ago?'

Carter was about to protest but the detective held up his hand and continued, 'Furthermore, the gentleman he flew to the island, as well as his lady companion, left the island, by sea, at least a fortnight ago, bound for Miami.' He sat back, the better to observe the reaction. Let's see him talk his way out of that, he thought.

'What?' Carter was flabbergasted. 'That is preposterous,' and then he thought of Ponce. Had he spread that rumour to stop anyone investigating their disappearance?

Jamison saw the look of doubt. Got him, he thought. 'Now, Mr er, Carter, shall we begin again. What is your name?'

There was a knock at the door. Jamison was annoyed at being interrupted just when he was about to get a confession. A young policeman entered, whispered something in the officer's ear.

He looked up, frowned, turned back to Carter saying, 'If you will excuse me for a moment.' He smiled politely, rose and left the room.

The interruption, to Carter, was one more trick to upset him.

What now? Is this meant to intimidate me? Surely Ponce isn't here to give evidence against me?

Carter could feel his resolution to remain calm slipping from him. If someone didn't start believing in him soon he would not be responsible for his actions. He put his head in his hands and tried to remember the relaxing exercises he had learnt at Meherabad.

'Would you please accompany me, Sir?' The detective had returned and indicated that that he wished Carter to follow him.

What is happening? Are they going to torture me? Surely not. They are part of the Commonwealth. What about Veronica? What have they done to her?

Carter had never known real fear before. He tried to stand but his legs betrayed him. He felt faint but fought against it. Should he shout, resist or just submit, and wait and see? If only he knew what was going on.

The other officer stood and came to help him. He took a deep breath, straightened his shoulders. He must stay strong if only for Veronica's sake.

He was led along a passage back to the front desk. Standing there was the last person in the world he had expected to see.

'Minty!'

They ran towards each other and nearly collided as they embraced. He kept repeating, 'Minty, Minty,' like a small child and she kept saying 'Carter, Carter, what has happened to you.' Everyone else stood back and watched the reunion.

After a time Martin joined them, holding out his hand. 'Hello, old man.

You seem to have got yourself into a spot of bother.'

Inspector Jamison thought the reunion had gone on long enough. There had obviously been some gigantic stuff up and the sooner he got to the bottom of it the sooner the whole incident would become nothing more than another island story.

'Mrs Stratton, I take it that you are willing to vouch for this man? That he is, in fact Carter, Roger, Langford'

'Oh yes, Inspector, this is indeed my darling boy.'

'And your relationship to this man is?'

'I am the closest thing he has to a mother. I have known and cared for him since the age of two. I can assure you that, as soon as he has a shave and haircut, he will look exactly like the photo on his passport.'

'Trouble is Minty, my passport went up in smoke along with everything else.'

'Went up in smoke?' Minty turned to Jamison.

Had the Inspector's skin been lighter it would have turned quite red. 'I think, Mr and Mrs Stratton there has been quite a mix up. If you would all come this way we will try to clear it up.' Then turning to the officer at the desk. 'If Sonny Millar is still around bring him to Number 2 interview room. If he has left, get him back.' Jamison was seething.

Someone was going to pay for this mess and it wasn't going to be him.

'Wait a minute,' Carter interrupted, folding his arms. 'I'm not budging until I see Veronica. If anything has happened to her I'm going to raise hell.'

'Veronica?' Minty looked from Carter to Jamison.

'Yes, Veronica,' Carter said. 'She is the woman who was with me and, Minty, she is the most wonderful person in the world. You will love her when you meet her.'

Minty smiled. Carter had poured his heart out to her more than once. Was this another passing fancy or was this the one? She rather hoped she would be, but changed her mind when a bedraggled, oddly attired, bewildered looking woman, was brought to join the group.

*   *   *

Veronica had just about lost touch with reality. What she had thought of as a rescue had turned into a nightmare. She had spent the entire night going over and over the events from the previous day and each time they seemed to be more bizarre than the last time. She had heard stories of English people disappearing in foreign countries, never to be heard of again. But surely these people were civilized? They spoke English.

When she was taken from her cell she thought it was for interrogation, *do they torture people here?* And the sight of Carter surrounded by people did nothing to allay her fears. *Are we being to be taken out and shot?*

She fainted.

Carter rushed to her aid and caught her before she hit the floor. 'What have you done to her?' he demanded.

'I assure you we have done nothing to upset her,' Jamison said, as the two men helped her to a bench. 'Someone, get water,' he shouted. 'If anyone had molested this woman in any way, I will have their head.'

Veronica revived, resting her head on Carter's shoulder. There was pandemonium all around but Carter was there. He would protect her.

Jamison became aware that the room was filling up, people coming from everywhere to see what was going on. He had to restore order before someone notified the press.

'If you are feeling well enough Miss, we were just about to go to the interview room and sort all this out. Do you feel well enough to accompany us?'

'It's all right Veronica. Don't be afraid, they know who we are. They're not going to hurt us.'

'Are you sure?'

'Yes, even Minty's here.'

And then she saw that there were people other than police in the room, including a middle aged woman who waved and gave her a brave smile. She lent on Carter's arm as he gently guided her towards a door being held open for her. More chairs were brought in and soon they were all sitting in a semicircle, facing a chastened Inspector Jamison.

'Mr Carter, it appears we owe you an apology. But the facts remain. Your appearance and attire were not usual for a guest at Polly Cay and the destruction on the island suggested that something out of the ordinary had happened. Could you now, in your own words, give us all a reasonable explanation for these events?'

'It will be my pleasure. But I must warn you it is a complicated story. Where should I begin?' He explained first, as best he could, the reason for his visit. 'I know it all sounds a bit farfetched but, both Mr Carter and Trevor thought my life was in imminent danger. That is why I left under such unusual circumstances.'

Now came to the difficult part. How could he explain drugging Ponce and his friend? Had they committed a crime? And should he tell the whole story or just the salient points. He decided to follow the latter course but not to tell any lies, if asked directly.

He explained his misgivings when Ponce and his friend arrive on the island. 'I was wary, and that is why I drugged him and his companion. It was as well that I did as I later learned that he had meant to do the same to me. When they recovered they could not find us so left because there was a storm, but they returned and searched the island. When they still couldn't find us they fired the island. Since then we have been surviving there as best we could. We thought, when you arrived, that you had come to save us and were horrified when we were arrested. My behaviour since then can be put down to my disappointment.'

'Your story seems to corroborate Miss Bell's account though hers was much more complicated and seemed to involve a gentleman called Manuel, but what is missing in both accounts is how you managed to conceal yourselves from your enemies.'

'Well, that was a stroke of luck. A day or so before, we had found a hurricane shelter. We hid in that.'

Jamison nodded. That made sense. 'One other thing, how do you explain a report that Miss Bell, and yourself had left the island by boat?'

'I have no idea but perhaps that was Ponce covering up what he had done. Who told you?'

'The same gentleman who failed to identify you this morning. He is the cause of all this misunderstanding, I've already sent for him and I intend making his life a misery for the next few days.'

There were formalities to go through and papers to be signed but eventually they were given permission to leave.

'A good hotel, a hot bath and a sleep might be the order of the day, I think,' Martin said as they signed the last paper.

'And a visit to the nearest hairdressers and dress shop,' Veronica added.

However, when they exited the station they were met with a barrage of reporters and cameras. The word had got out about the goings on inside. Reporters fired questions at them, others wrote in notebooks and cameras flashed. Despite their strange appearance it appears that they were English. The appearance of Minty and Martin added credence to this. Martin had to become quite aggressive trying to protect Minty from a young reporter who kept thrusting a microphone into her face. Eventually they forced their way to a waiting taxi, organised by Inspector Jamison.

This time Veronica and Carter were again photographed, in their wild state, by a TV camera crew. They were still hot news. It was a slack news day, so garbled accounts of what had happened appeared on Nassau local television, but also on the BBC.

CHAPTER 22

Carter Found

Reggie was much too busy to head off, himself, on what might turn out to be a wild goose chase, so he sent a man, post haste to Nassau to find this Raymond Miller and get the full story.

He also remembered that Merv had had a younger sister who married a Scotsman. It did not take him long to find out that she was now living in Aberdeen, so went, himself, to find his old friend, Curtis.

She was overjoyed to see him. 'Oh, Mr Pike, of course I remember you and I am oh, so glad that you came. Mervin has been seriously ill, double pneumonia they say. He was delirious for days and kept raving about someone called Carter, and another named Neighsmith, and goodness knows what else. In his delirium he thought he was still running his old law firm.

'Even when the worst of the fever was passed he kept goin' on so and, as it seemed to upset him so much, the doctors have kept him, sedated. They say his mind just needs to rest, but I'm thinkin' there is something on his mind that will not let him rest.'

Reggie knew he had the answer but did not want to frighten the woman.

'Dear Ellen, I think I know what is troubling him. Could you ask the doctors to cease the medication and let me speak to him?' And they'd better, he thought, or I'll sue them for malpractice.

It took a day of his precious time but he had left a very reliable man behind so only rang three times to check that everything was in order. The next morning he was shown into the private ward where Mervin Curtis was recovering.

Reggie was horrified at the appearance of his boyhood friend. *God, he looks like a centenarian and he's not more than a year older than myself.* He felt the first stirrings of his own mortality.

'Reggie, so good of you to visit. I'm afraid I have been under the weather for some time. My mind still seems to be in a bit clouded.'

'Don't stress yourself, boyo, but I'd like to know what you've done with my Veronica?'

'Veronica? Oh, yes, the girl. Are they not back? My god, what day is it, what week, what year?'

'Now calm down, man. It's about six weeks since they left.'

'Six weeks! And no-one's sent a message to tell them to come home?' Mervin tried to sit up. 'Send a message to a Trevor Jones at my old firm and tell him to come here at once. No, that will take too long. Get me a phone and I'll ring him at work.'

Mervin was rejuvenated. He could feel new energy coursing through his veins but Reggie thought that the excitement would kill his friend. 'Calm down, calm down. I've already sent a man to Nassau to find them.'

'So, you know all about it.' Mervin sighed and collapsed back onto the pillow.

'Well, I know where they went but what I want to know is, why did you send them there in the first place and what has that toad Neighsmith got to do with it?'

Mervin tried to sit up again. 'You mean Neighsmith senior?

'No, that idiot son. He's in an institution now, you know. But let's not get bogged down with him. I know how he was pissed off at not becoming the next Lord Alyward. What was he doing over there and why did you send my Veronica there in the first place?'

Mervin relaxed again. 'Then Carter is safe. All those dreadful things I thought about were only in my mind. They'll be fine there. They will have servants and everything and if the food is running out they can soon send out for more.

'The reason for their going, well it is a long story, but the nuts and bolts of it are that Carter is actually the late Lord Alywin's grandson. The old boy found it hard to accept that he had a grandson who was part Indian, but after all he was flesh and blood. He kept a weather eye on him and decided that he had grown to be quite a gentleman in spite of his origins.

'About a year before he died he had me draw up new a will, leaving everything to the boy so long as he remained of good character. Everything was to be kept secret for six months after the Lord's death but if he broke the law, even a drunk driving charge during that time, everything was to revert to the Neighsmiths. Somehow, they must have found out. I blame Kirkwood.

'Jones, Carter's friend, realised that they were trying to get Carter into trouble so I decided I would get him away from England until the six months was up.'

'But why didn't you just tell the boy to be careful?'

'Then it wouldn't have been a secret. I know that these days there is scant respect for the law but there a still a few of us who keep the faith.' Then he became quite agitated. 'How long is it since they left?'

'It's at least six weeks.'

Curtis gave a sigh of satisfaction and Reggie thought he could see energy flowing back into his friend. He seemed to become younger before his eyes.

'Then he is safe. Now, if you will help me to get up, I need to make a telephone call.'

'Are you sure you are up to walking?'

'Of course I am. I think my body has been ready for days. It was my mind that was misplaced. Now that I remember everything I need to act.'

With Reggie's assistance and in spite of protests from a nurse, Mervin managed to get to the public phone in the reception area and rang Trevor.

'Mr Curtis, where have you been? I've searched for you everywhere. There is so much to tell.'

'Time for that later. I want you to send a message straight away to a Raymond Miller in The Bahamas. It is time Carter came home.'

'He's already on his way, Sir. He will be here in a couple of days. Have you not seen the news?'

'News. I'm recovering in a hospital, not sitting in my lounge room.'

'Then, if you have access to a television set I would advise you to tune into Channel Four news in about … er, seven minutes.'

Curtis could not see the man at the end of the phone, but he could hear the suppressed laughter in his voice. 'What on earth for, boy?'

'I won't spoil the surprise, but I assure you it will be worth it.' Curtis could hear his laughter as he hung up.

'The boy's gone mad,' he informed Reggie. 'Wants me to watch the news.' Then, noticing that there was indeed a television set on the wall, he called out to the nervous nurse who was still hovering close by. 'Young woman, could you please turn on that contraption and put it on Channel Four. I need to watch the news.'

The reception left a lot to be desired but as a description of a devastating earthquake in Iran faded into a report of the resignation of B.J. Vorster in South Africa both men became impatient, but the next item grabbed their attention.

'And now we switch to the Bahamas where strange things are happening.' The camera switched to a tropical scene and then to the presented.

'This is Lesley Ley, of World News, reporting from Nassau. Yesterday, if you were listening, we reported that a strange, new cult was being set up on one of the lesser islands.' She held up an enlarged copy of the photo of a wild looking man that had appeared in the local paper. 'Today this strange case has taken a very different turn.' And the scene switched to that of four people leaving police headquarters.

The camera focused, first on Minty and Martin, extended to the whole group, then onto Carter and Veronica, still as they were when they had been brought to Nassau.

'This strange couple, who at first were thought to be the cult's leaders turn out to be two respectable English scientists, working on a remote Bahaman island and had been marooned on Polly Cay for the last six weeks.'

The broadcast went on but Reggie and Mervin were not listening. They were staring at the two persons on the screen. Curtis said, 'That's Carter,' while Pike pointed at the screen. 'Bloody hell, that's Veronica.'

They missed the rest of the news as both began making frantic arrangements to get back to London. When they read a more detailed account in the evening news they were somewhat mystified, but relieved that the couple were to be flown back to England in a day or two. Both men were anxious to be there when the couple arrived back in Britain.

Reggie was anxious to get Veronica home. Though his "girls" were his business, he felt a fatherly interest in their wellbeing. He wanted her safely home. If she had been harmed in any way, someone was going to pay.

Curtis was anxious to be the one to tell Carter of his new fortune. He would make it his business to be at Gatwick when he landed. In the meantime he would have a quiet word with Kirkwood. The business was no longer his but he still cherished its reputation. He intended giving the man a timely reminder about protecting client's rights, as he suspected that it was through Kirkwood, that the Neighsmiths had learnt of the terms of Lord Alyward's will.

CHAPTER 23

I Love You

As tourism is the main source of revenue for the Bahamas, it abounds in luxury resorts. On the taxi driver's advice the group were quickly installed in a nearby hotel which not only had on-suite rooms and magnificent beach views but amenities to pamper the most discerning of guests.

Martin had a little difficulty persuading the receptionist that Carter and Veronica were suitable clientele, but after he had spun a little lie suggesting that they were, in fact, scientists who had just participated in a nature documentary, they became welcome guests.

Veronica had caught a glimpse of herself in the large mirror in the foyer. She was horrified. How could she have become this hideous in six weeks? Minty assured her that an hour or so of pampering with the full spa treatment would work wonders. Then they would investigate hairdressers and fashion houses.

Carter was content with a long, soak in the on-suite bath and then a good sleep. Later in the day he borrowed a shirt and slacks from Martin and visited the hotel barber, who was horrified when he requested a short haircut.

'But Mon,' the barber insisted, 'such curls. It would be sacrilege to cut them. I could fluff them up for a fuller Afro, or dreads. Mon you would have dreads to rival Bob Marley.'

'Thank you for the compliment but just short back and sides, perhaps a little thicker on top, will suit me fine.'

The young man complied, sighing as first one then another curly, black lock fell to the floor. 'And now the beard, Mon? Surely you will leave the beard?'

Carter inspected his chin. It was rather luxurious, he thought. 'Oh well, perhaps I'll keep it for a while. Just tidy it up.'

He was quite pleased with the final result. It rather suited his darker skin. Feeling like a man reborn he and Martin had a drink to celebrate then set out to buy an outfit suitable for this new person.

Both parties had agreed to meet in the foyer for drinks before dinner. Carter was looking forward to showing off the new "he" to Veronica, but as the time grew closer he became apprehensive. Now that the ordeal was over would she even want to see him?

The plane had arrived before he had had time to tell her of the revelation he had had. He hadn't even had time to tell her how much he loved her, how she was indispensable to the rest of his life. He wished they were back on the island, at least long enough to tell her of his love. He had no idea how she felt about him. Perhaps the experience had been so frightening that she would never want to see him again. What if she rejected him, before he even had a chance to prove to her that he was a worthwhile person?

Minty and Veronica had spent the preceding hours getting the full beauty treatment then went shopping. When they walked into the foyer they could have graced the covers of any social magazine. Minty had never felt so elegant and Veronica was again the glamorous young woman she had been before the forced sojourn on the island. But as she walked towards the waiting men her new found confidence dissipated.

How would Carter feel about her now? They had shared such an intimate time together. She had shed all pretence. She believed she had been his friend, his equal, but how would he regard her now? Would he want to continue this relationship or was she still nothing more than a hired companion? She looked at him, trying to guess his mood but he seemed to be sending mixed messages.

Carter was as confused as she was. He wanted to rush forward and embrace her, hold her and pour out his love for her, but what would be her reaction? Was he still nothing more than a customer? And if she did accept his declaration, what did he have to offer her. She had mixed with powerful, intelligent men. He wasn't powerful and he had never been praised for his intelligence. Could being slightly more than competent cricketer compete with a poet or a captain of industry? He knew his heart would break if she rejected him.

In the end he reverted to the humorous banter that had sustained them on the island. 'Behold the princess reborn,' he declared.

Well, if that was how he wants it, I can certainly play that game, she thought. 'As if it isn't the gallant Sea Hawk, the scourge of the Caribbean? Mr Flynn, I presume.'

'Do you think so?' Carter smiled, stroking his chin and then, turning to his friends. 'May I introduce the beautiful Donna Marie.'

Of course Minty and Martin already knew who Veronica was but they went along with the farce. And so, the mood was set. They joked their way through the meal but even Minty, who wasn't the quickest to recognise a strained situation, sensed that something else was going on. Later, in their own room, she discussed it with her husband.

'Did you feel that we were actors in some badly written parlour romp tonight, Martin?'

'Darling, even someone newly arrived from Mars could feel it. I don't know what has gone on between those two. They were like two people walking on cracked ice tonight, but there is nothing we can do Minty. They are adults and they will have to work it out for themselves. We will just have to stand by and cheer them on, or pick up the pieces, when they finally work out what their relationship is. Now come to bed. You can't save the world every day.'

'I know Martin but she seems such a nice girl and it's time Carter settled down. I do want him to have a happy life.'

'Spoken like a good mother but, as I said before, they've got to work it out for themselves'

They stayed in Nassau two more days but neither Veronica nor Carter would make the first move to renew the relationship that had developed on the island. They were like two teenagers dancing around a romance, each afraid to make the first move.

*   *   *

There was yet one more bizarre incident that occurred before they left the island. Reggie had sent his man to The Bahamas before he had learnt the whole story from Curtis. This man had not bothered to watch TV or read newspapers. He had been sent to find a Raymond Miller and find him he did.

Poor Raymond was only beginning to absorb the shock of learning of Sonny's dereliction of duty and the trouble it had caused to, not only Carter and his friend, but to Inspector Jamison. He felt his son's failure was a family disgrace. They had served the Alywards for generations. Now, through the neglect of his son, not only had guests been abused, but the structures on the island had been destroyed. The fact that he had been the one to notify the police of the destruction on the island, only added to his misery.

It was not just that he might lose the contract that had sustained the family in hard times for so long, though that was a real worry, it was the disgrace of letting Lord Alyward down. He was sitting in his small lounge room contemplating his future when a taxi pulled up, a large man jumped out and pounded on the front door.

The door was rather fragile. Raymond hurried to open it before the man knocked again.

'Are you Raymond Miller?' the man demanded.

'Yes, sur, yes,' was the frightened reply.

'Where's Veronica Bell.'

'Veronica Bell?'

'Yes. Stop foolin' around and tell me where she is?'

Raymond tried to stem the rising panic he felt. 'Please, please Sur, this lady. I do not think I know this lady.'

'Don't give me that rubbish. You took her out to that island along with a fella. Is she still there?'

'Ah, Sur, I do know the lady, at least I know of her. It was my son who took her out to da island, but I do know of her where'bouts. She was recently at the police station but now is visitin' with her friend in town.'

'What do you mean, police station. Why the bloody hell was she there?'

'Ah' sur, it is a long story, but I can see you are a busy mon. It was all a case of mistaken identity. But all is not lost. If you go to police headquarters and ask for Inspector Jamison, he's da man who can give you all de details and de present abode of the young lady. But on behalf of all de people of Bahama I offer you an apology and, when you see the lady please give her my apologies too.'

If he thought it would have helped, Raymond would have gone on his knees to deliver his speech. He also promised himself that when he next saw Sonny he would give him a tongue lashing. He almost wished that it was still a time when a father could give his son a real lashing just as the old masters used to do.

Reggie's man was not sure about involving police in his boss' affairs so thought he would send a cable and wait for further orders.

*   *   *

Because they were still big news, Carter and Veronica had tried to keep a low profile during their stay, letting Minty or Martin deal with any contact with the public so, two days later, they waited in the departure lounge until it was time to board their plane for home. It was one of the few times that they had been alone since the island.

Carter felt it would be his last chance to speak his mind, but how to begin? Veronica was also wanting to say something, but what? If only he would give her some sign.

'Well,' he said letting out a big sigh, 'the adventure ends.'

Veronica looked at him. His eyes seemed to say one thing but his words said something else. Was she just imagining it or was he still stalling? I can't stand the suspense any longer, she thought, so here goes.

'Was it just an adventure, Carter? Is that all it was to you?'

'Hell, no.' *Is she offering me an opening or is it just my imagination?* 'It was a lot more than that.' He took another deep breath. *In for a penny.*

'No Veronica, it was not an adventure. It was the most wonderful time in my whole life. You must think me the greatest of all idiots and I will understand if you laugh in my face, but Veronica, I love you. I love you with every fibre in my being. I never want to spend another day without you. Do you have some feeling for me?'

He had such a look of longing in his eyes it nearly broke her heart. She opened her arms to comfort him.

'Oh, Carter, of course I love you.' She wanted to say more but he was already kissing her, her face, her hair, her lips. She felt like water in his arms as he murmured over and over, 'I love you, I love you. Oh, Veronica, my dearest one, I love you.'

And that is how they were when Minty and Martin came to collect them. They stood to one side for a time, unwilling to disturb them, but boarding time was close.

'I'm sorry to interrupt,' Martin said, 'but it's time to go.'

They disengaged but stood like two people still in a dream.

'Congratulations,' Minty said, 'It's about time, Carter. I thought you'd never pluck up the courage to declare yourself.'

He laughed. 'Was it that obvious?' His grin was as bright as sunrise as he turned to them. 'Minty, Martin, allow me to introduce my future wife,' and then he had a moment's doubt. 'You do want to marry me don't you Veronica?'

'Of course I do,' she laughed. 'As soon as you ask me.'

'Ask? Oh yes!' *Should I get down on one knee?* 'Veronica Bell, will you do the honour of becoming my wife?'

'Of course I will, Darling.'

And they embraced again. The departure lounge was filling up by this time but they had not noticed and were surprised when loud applause greeted her acceptance. They were embarrassed but delighted at the well wishes that followed them as they walked hand in hand towards the waiting plane.

CHAPTER 24

Lord of Saylewood

The flight out to Nassau had been filled with expectation. They were going on an adventure and they were anxious for it to begin. The flight back was different. When they were back on the ground neither of them knew what their new lives would hold. There would be decisions to make, new lives to plan, a time to try and make some sense of what had happened on Polly Cay.

This flight was a respite between the past and the future. Veronica and Carter sat together, holding hands, saying little. They ordered drinks, meals only because they were requested. There were earphones which offered a choice of music or news broadcasts, an overhead television showing the latest movie, but they ignored them. They left their seats only when nature demanded and spoke to Minty and Martin only when spoken to.

The flight out had seemed so long but, this time the aeroplane seemed to be eating up the miles, though in fact the return journey was two hours longer. They did not want to land, fearing that the world would intrude into their newfound happiness and yet they knew it could not begin until then.

But every journey has an ending and, all too soon, they were being ordered to 'please take your seats, put on your seat belts and prepare for landing'. They felt the planes' decent and saw the fluffy mattress of clouds change to a slate blue sky, and then to grey sea and finally child sized buildings, which grew larger as the plane descended.

As soon as they came to a stop, people were cheering, clapping, standing, overhead lockers clicking open and bodies were pushing into the aisle, everyone anxious to stand on English soil. Soon attendants had created order out of the chaos and an orderly line, for which the English were famous, formed and began to move forward to exit the aeroplane.

Only Carter and Veronica sat, still holding hands.

'Come on you two, time to disembark.'

Minty was already fussing, checking that she had all her possessions, but Martin seemed to understand their reticence. 'Time to face the future.'

Carter gave Veronica's hand a squeeze and stood up. 'Here we are darling. I guess it is all finally over. Back to reality. At least we will now get a proper explanation for what went on. And this time we can face it together.'

Veronica smiled, gave him her hand, then standing, remembered who she was and began checking her hair, her skirt and wished she had gone to the toilet and checked her makeup.

There was quite a reception committee waiting to meet them in the terminal. Curtis, a renewed man, full of energy, had not only made the journey to London and given his warning to Kirkwood, but had established, beyond doubt, that Carter's inheritance was now a legal fact. He was determined that he would be the one to impart the news to the boy he had watched grow to manhood. He felt a fatherly pride in him.

Reggie had brought along quite a welcoming home contingent to bolster up Veronica's spirit, should the adventure have damaged her ego. Remembering the picture he had seen on T.V. he was worried what would confront him at the terminal. He knew her appearance could be easily rectified but what would it have done to her ego? He had brought the gang along to give her moral support and convince her that she was just as lovable as before.

An enterprising reporter in Nassau had discovered that the so called, "Tarzan and Mate," were on the flight and notified his London office. A TV crew were anxiously awaiting their arrival. They also wanted to be the first to welcome them home and get the scoop of the week.

None of the other passengers had realised that the attractive couple sitting quietly in their seats were, in fact, the two who had made headlines a couple of days before, so were mystified by the crowd at reception, and a little annoyed when they were having difficulty finding their own friends or family, but most hung around to discover who the V.I.P. might be.

Two or three times the camera had panned the disembarking crowd but nobody out of the ordinary seemed to be exiting. Surely there would be a reception committee to meet these scientists who had been through such a harrowing time? Could it all be a giant hoax? Perhaps they should just pack up and head home?

Minty and Martin had waited until Carter and Veronica finally left the plane, consequently they were the last four to pass through customs into the terminal. By that time many of the onlookers had given up waiting and the camera crew were packing up. Even Reggie was beginning to think that someone had stuffed up, but Curtis waited and because he also knew Minty, was the first to spot them. He waved as he pushed himself, rather rudely, to the front.

Carter saw him and felt an overwhelming gratitude for the man who had been there, at every turn in his life, to offer encouragement, advice and direction.

'Look, Veronica, there's Mr Curtis,' and he left her side to hurry forward and embrace his friend. He was shocked as he felt the frailty of the man, and shame that he had so neglected this person, who had been so important in his life.

'My boy, welcome back.' Curtis left aside his usual reserve and joined wholeheartedly in the hug.

Veronica moved towards the pair expecting to be introduced, so was close enough to hear his next words.

'Carter, my boy, let me be the first to congratulate you. You are now the new Lord of Saylewood.'

'The Lord of Saylewood? I don't understand.'

'It will all be official when the will is read but you are Lord Alyward's heir and Saylewood was his estate.'

'But why?'

'He was your grandfather, boy.'

'My grandfather! That man was my grandfather? The one who disinherited my father? Yet he has left me his estate? I don't understand.'

Veronica did not hear all of this conversation but she had heard enough to know that Carter was now a peer of the realm. She stepped aside. This would make all the difference. As Mrs Carter Langford her former occupation would mean nothing but Lady Langford would never be accepted in certain circles. She might even bump into former clients. The bottom had just fallen out of the new wonderful world she had hardly entered.

'Veronica, welcome home.' A big man with a booming voice was giving her a great bear hug. She was bewildered until she realised that it was Reggie.

'Reggie, oh Reggie, thank god you've come.' She clung to him as to a life raft.

He was instantly concerned. 'Veronica, girl, is something wrong? Are you OK?'

'Yes, yes. It's just that it has all been too much. Take me home, please, now.' She was close to tears.

'OK, Darling. Don't fret yourself. We'll get a cab to my place. You can rest there and we'll deal with all this later.'

When Carter had finally absorbed the news of his parentage and elevation into the ranks of privilege he remembered Veronica and turned to introduce her to Mr Curtis but she was gone.

CHAPTER 25
Polly Cay

'Veronica, Veronica. Where are you?' Carter shouted, stretching his neck to see and pushing the people around him out of the way. She wasn't behind him and he couldn't see her in the crowd that had heard the glad tidings and were pushing forward to offer their congratulations. They were not quite sure what it was all about but, no doubt, it would be in the news. They would be able to boast to their friends that they were there when it happened. They might even get into the news themselves. Carter pushed them aside as he strode through the terminal looking for Veronica.

Outside passengers had formed queues waiting as taxis drove through in an orderly line. The wait infuriated Reggie but he knew that there was nothing he could do. He might be an influential man but at the taxi rank he was just another passenger.

Finally, he reached the head of the queue. The next taxi was his. He was just about to open the door for Veronica when he heard a voice shouting, 'Veronica.'

He turned to see a young man run towards her. 'Veronica. Thank God I've found you.' He reached for her hand.

Reggie stood, still holding the door.

'Do you want this taxi or not?' the driver demanded.

He was torn between claiming his ride or rescuing Veronica. 'Wait a minute.'

'Can't do that. Can't hold up the line. Either you get in or it's the next customer.'

What was the good of the taxi without Veronica, and who the hell was that man? He surrendered the car which was quickly claimed by the next in the queue. He had no idea who the young man was, but Veronica was his responsibility. She might need him.

Veronica had turned when she heard Carter calling her name. In a stride he was by her side and grabbed her hand.

'Why did you leave? Where are you going?'

'Oh, Carter. I just wanted to get away. It will be easier that way.'

'Easier? What do you mean?'

'Carter, it's all over. It was really only a dream and now it will be impossible.'

'Impossible. What do you mean? Was all that you said in the waiting room a lie? Don't you love me anymore?'

'It's got nothing to do with love Carter. We can't marry now.'

'Now? What's different? You said you loved me. You said you would marry me. What has happened to change that?'

Veronica could see the pain in his eyes. She had meant to just walk away but she couldn't leave him hurting like this.

'Carter, when you asked me to marry you, you were just Carter Langford. Now you're a Lord. You could never marry me now.'

'Why not. What's being a Lord got to do with it?'

'Carter, if I married you I would become a Lady, a part of the English peerage. I'd be a very visible part of society and just think what a picnic the press would have with that. Not to mention your fellow Lords and Ladies.'

'Do you mean that we can't be married because of a stupid title?' He was angry and turned her, rather roughly, towards him just as Reggie arrive to rescue her.

'Veronica is this man molesting you?' he demanded.

'No Reggie, it's all right.'

She turned back to Carter. She had never been ashamed of what she did. It wasn't as if she went around soliciting or sold herself to the highest bidder. What she was doing was probably much more honest than the future her mother had planned for her. But she knew society wouldn't see it that way.

'Yes Carter. That is just what I'm saying. When you think about it you will see it too. I am not a suitable person to be your wife.'

'Not suitable? You are not only the most suitable, you are the only one who could ever be my wife. What do I care about a stupid title? I never asked for it in the first place.'

'Carter, think. You are all emotional at present, but when you have got used to the idea you will think more clearly. You can't just walk away from all this.'

'Then, you don't really love me?'

She was shocked at the look of desolation in his eyes. She couldn't hurt him anymore. 'Of course I love you, Carter. I never thought I could love anyone like this but it will never work.'

'So, you do love me.'

She saw a light come back into his eyes. 'And the only reason why you will not marry me is because a stupid old man thought he could sooth his conscience by leaving me his title? But don't you know that you're worth more to me that any title.'

'Carter, are you saying that you would give it all up for me?'

'Yes, yes. He can keep his mansion and his millions and his stupid old title. I never wanted it in the first place. He disinherited my father. Well, I'm disinheriting him. I only wish he was here so I could say it to his face.'

'Carter, are you sure? You don't think you will regret it later?'

'Veronica, stop doubting me. Remember I am a man of my word.' His expression became serious. 'Veronica Bell, will you do me the honour of becoming my wife? Please.' The love shining in his eyes was like a bolt of electricity. She felt her knees go weak.

'Oh, Carter, yes.' She fell into his open arms and they were both blinded by the bolt of lightning that flashed between them.

'Boy, that one will make the papers for sure.'

A cameraman, who had been alerted to a possible scoop by Carter's dash through the terminal, had run after him. He was very happy that he had.

They laughed when they realised that the earth had not exploded.

Reggie, who had witnessed everything, sprang forward. 'How dare you take photos without asking permission? Give me that camera at once,' and he made a grab for it.

Veronica intervened. 'Leave him Reggie,' and then to the man, 'Could you send me a copy?' Then she drew Reggie into the group. 'Come and be meet my intended husband, Reggie. This wonderful man is willing to give up his inheritance just to marry me.'

'Well, almost all,' Carter paused. 'I have got one reservation, Veronica.' He smiled when he saw the look of doubt.

'I will give up the title and Saylewood and everything else, Ponce's dad can have the lot, but I will keep one place. I want Polly Cay for myself. I want to keep the place that brought us together. I want to restore it, make it better than it was before.'

'And then, what will you do with it, Carter?' Veronica asked.

'Why, I'll turn it into a hide-away for newlyweds.'

Then he had a better idea. 'Veronica, what do you say we leave England and run a luxury hideaway for honeymooners?'

HONEYMOON HIDEAWAY

POLLY CAY

A Garden of Eden just meant for two

On Polly Cay we have four, isolated,
self-contained, fully serviced bungalows.
You can spend all day swimming in pristine blue water,
walking on sun-drenched sands,
lying back and watching magnificent sunsets
and never be disturbed by another human being,
Or
Share a great variety of activities at the

HOME PLANTATION

Snorkeling, Fishing, Paddle Boarding, Golf Putting, Cruising the Island

And

The Evening Banquet and Entertainment

Every day's a holiday on Polly Cay

www.ingramcontent.com/pod-product-compliance
Lightning Source LLC
Chambersburg PA
CBHW070025120726
47909CB00003B/1063